I0603195

DISCOVERED

BECA LEWIS

PERCEPTION PUBLISHING

CONTENTS

ONE

*I*t *should have been beautiful,* Suzanne thought as she approached Aaron's Palace. But instead, it was barren, empty, and ugly. Aaron had stripped the land so that the Palace and all its glitter would be the only thing people would see. Aaron and his greed were on display.

She was exhausted. The trip from the Islands of Lopel and Hetale had taken much longer than she had expected. Her envy of other shapeshifters that could be anything had reared its ugly head more than once during the trip.

She thought she had gotten rid of that envy long ago. But as she traveled, Suzanne thought how much easier it would have been if she could shapeshift into something other than a dragon.

If she could turn into a mouse, she could have traveled with Bolong's crown of dragons through time and arrived days ahead. She could have hidden away beneath one of their wings, Sawdi none the wiser that they had a stowaway.

But no. She had to be only a dragon—a very distinctive one at that. In the earth realm, she had often passed as a pileated woodpecker, and that red stripe on her head remained even here on this god-forsaken planet, Thamon.

God-forsaken was the right term for it. It had been god-forsaken ever since Aaron, Stryker, and Sawdi decided to make up a religion, turn Aaron into a God, and banish all other gods and even magic of all kinds. Yes, god-forsaken, but hopefully not for long.

She and the rest of the rebellion were ready to fight. She hoped nothing significant had happened while she flew to the continent of Edes where Aaron lived. Stryker and his crown of dragons and Warrior Monks were so far ahead of her they had time to prepare whatever they were going to do next. Their trip had been easy, unlike hers.

Suzanne's trip to Aaron's palace was exhausting. Not only because of how far away it was but because she had to travel without being seen. All dragons except Sawdi's were killed on sight, no questions asked.

But the journey was so long, many times she needed to stop to rest on islands, or even rocks, that jutted out of the ocean. She tried to pick places where no one was living, but sometimes that wasn't possible. Ironically, her last stop had been the one that almost did her in. She thought it was a deserted strip of land, but had spotted a group of people right before landing. But she had no choice; she was too exhausted to keep flying. The people saw her and started pointing and yelling.

She had no idea if they were pointing because they were planning to report her to the local Kai-Via or simply because they hadn't seen a dragon for so long that they were curious. Either way, after she landed, she quickly shifted back to being a woman and ran into the woods and hid for the rest of the day, sleeping within a cavity of a tree.

That night, under cover of darkness, she stole food from one of the farmers, wishing she had something to leave in return. She had consoled herself, saying that she was on a mission to free these people from the tyranny of Aaron-Lem.

She hoped that if they knew that they would have fed her. Still, she couldn't take any chances, because at the moment most of the people on the planet of Thamon were completely under Aaron-Lem's spell.

2

She had thought she would see some evidence that people were revolting. Aaron's new decree commanded that the people give him all their gold and jewels and a large portion of what they earned either as craftspeople or farmers. But on that tiny slip of land, there was no sign of rebellion. Perhaps Aaron hadn't gotten to them yet to ask for anything.

Suzanne made a quick pass over the Palace, flying high enough that she hoped no one would see her. After getting her bearings and locating the cave where Bolong had told her he and his friends lived, she flew over a low range of hills a few miles from the Palace and descended into the woods behind them, praying that no one saw her.

Suzanne hoped that if she were spotted, since they were so close to the Palace, they would think that she was one of Sawdi's dragons. Except that Sawdi's dragons remained dragons and would never turn into a person, let alone a woman.

Bolong had shared the story of how he and the other four dragons had been placed under a spell by Sawdi a long time ago. Now they would be men, or so they assumed, having never been able to shapeshift again.

The only people who would know that she wasn't part of Sawdi's crown of dragons were Sawdi or Aaron. Hopefully, neither one of them was nearby. They are too busy plotting evil, Suzanne thought as she started walking towards the cave.

If Sawdi or Aaron had walked the woods once in a while and listened to the animals that lived there, perhaps they might not have turned into the men they were today. Where she came from, everyone knew that magic and nature were intertwined, and they lived within the harmony of that awareness.

Well, most people. Her sister, Meg, had been too busy being full of herself to notice and had run away to Thamon. Now they were in Thamon where magic was banned. And instead of harmony, there was the fake god Aaron and his false religion of Aaron-Lem.

She had plenty of time to think as she traveled across the ocean to join forces with the dragons and the other rebels waiting for a revolution to begin.

On the Islands they had already begun, and won, their revolution, giving them hope that they would succeed on the rest of the planet.

Now that tiny band of rebels had split up. Many of the rescued Mages had stayed to protect the Islands after saving them from Sawdi and the Warrior Monks. It was their magic that had helped cloak the people of the Islands when the Warrior Monks had come looking for them.

Ibris, the Preacher, and Dax, the head of the Islands' Kai-Via, stayed too. Having been the ones who helped convert the people in the first place, they knew they needed to stay and support the people as they adjusted to living without Aaron-Lem. It would not be an easy task.

A few of the rebels had taken some of the survivors of the prison camp to the Sanctuary on Turva. It was where some people, following the warnings of the prophecies, had gone to hide before Aaron-Lem took over. At least Suzanne hoped that was where they were.

Of course, Stryker had betrayed them all. He thought he had outwitted them by running away. But he was wrong. They had set him up to run so that Sawdi and the Warrior Monks would leave the Islands and go after him.

Suzanne ducked under a tree branch and thought about how the last few months had been filled with betrayals, twists, and turns. She knew that wasn't over yet. There would be more.

In the meantime, Stryker was heading to where he thought he would find the next part of the pendant. The rest of the rebels, including Suzanne's sister, were on Captain Lira's ship, the Eos, trying to get to the pendant before Stryker. Her job was to find

Bolong and get caught up on what had happened since she saw him last. Then they had their own rebellion to plan.

But first, rest. Because no matter what Bolong told her about what was happening, and how anxious they were to begin, she needed to rest first.

Two

Once again, Stryker was on a ship, and he hated ships. They rolled with the waves. They smelled. They were filled with Ordinary men. But most of all, they were slow. And he was in a hurry.

If he could access his power to transport himself, he would. But he couldn't. He told himself that it was because he didn't want to reveal that he had some magical powers. After all, he was responsible for banning magic and killing Mages and shapeshifters everywhere he found them. He couldn't let on that he had some magical ability.

Not much, to be sure. But some. Or at least he used to. Now he wasn't so sure, and he was having a hard time admitting that to himself.

Once, a long time ago, he had transported himself somewhere. It had been such a thrill he had wanted to repeat it, and never could as hard as he tried. Now he wondered if he had actually ever transported himself at all.

Was it because he hadn't practiced, or because he didn't have that ability or any magic at all? Both thoughts were disturbing, and either way, he was stuck on the Soleis as it traveled slowly across the ocean to where the map was leading him.

He wasn't going to bother stopping at Aaron's palace to attempt to make peace with him and Sawdi. Because once he had the last piece of the pendant, it wouldn't matter if he had magic or not.

He could use the pendant's power to control everyone, including Sawdi and his Warrior Monks. No, he was going straight to Turva, where the map had shown him that he would find the final piece of the pendant.

The idea that everyone, including Aaron and that freak Sawdi, would be under his power, was enough to make Stryker almost forget how much he hated ships. Almost.

But this ship was going so slow he could swear that it was going around in circles. He hadn't remembered that it had taken this long to get from Aaron's Palace to the Islands of Lopel and Hetale before.

Maybe it felt slower because last time he had that cook and his men making him food and waiting on him. This time, he was on a different ship, and Captain Kosti made his food, and it was the crew that served him.

Although he still demanded that one of the men taste his food first, it was not what he was used to, and as much as he threatened them, it didn't make any difference. Captain Kosti said that they hadn't been expecting Stryker and had not prepared anything special.

That was true. Kosti hadn't been expecting him. Being on the Soleis was a last-minute lucky escape from the rebels on Lopel.

Yes, he had betrayed the people on the Islands. Why not? He was sure they would have betrayed him if they had a chance to. Karn had hidden the second part of the pendant from him with the promise that if Stryker helped them defeat Sawdi and his Warrior Monks, they would give it to him.

But he hadn't waited and hadn't helped. When the map showed him where that shapeshifter had hidden the pendant piece, he grabbed it and ran. Falcon had secured the ship for him, and they had left the Islands just before Sawdi arrived, and a massive storm swept over the Islands.

Between Sawdi, the Warrior Monks, and the storm, Stryker figured the people on the Islands were probably dead. Hopefully, at least the rebels were killed. How could they have escaped the fury of those three things?

But a tiny part of Stryker hoped that a few of them had survived. The ones that he had trained, Ibris, Dax, and even Karn. They were his boys. Even though he had betrayed them too, he would miss them. But, once he had the pendant, he wouldn't need preachers, warriors, or the Kai-Via.

A huge rolling wave passed under the Soleis, and Stryker grabbed the nearest post to keep from falling. He swore under his breath. Yes, he hated ships, and he hated this one the most.

****

As Stryker struggled on the deck of the Soleis, Falcon and Captain Kosti mind-spoke to each other. Although Stryker thought that his being on the Soleis had been random luck, it wasn't. Kosti, Karn, and Falcon had planned it.

However, there was one thing that Stryker was right about. Yes, the Soleis was barely getting anywhere. Instead of a straight line to the continent of Turva, they were going in slow spirals. The spirals were small enough that it looked as if they were always heading in the right direction. But they were moving as slowly as possible in the process.

Stryker was also correct in that the waves were worse than he remembered, thanks to careful steering by the crew. All of them were enjoying Stryker's discomfort and did everything they could to make it worse.

Kosti and Falcon were old friends or had been when Falcon was a boy—before Sawdi turned him into a Falcon and gifted him to Stryker. Kosti had also been at Stryker's training camp for boys, but had escaped one night and never looked back. He had been sailing the seas ever since. For years he had done his best to stay away from anything to do with Aaron-Lem.

But when Falcon approached him and his crew to help him, Kosti couldn't say no. All he had to do was make sure it took Stryker a long time to get to Turva.

It was Karn Kolbe who had made the arrangements with Falcon long before he had gone to the Islands to help his wife, Wren, and the rest of the rebels.

If Stryker knew how many of his past students were now fighting against him, he would not have believed it. He thought he had trained them to serve only him. What he didn't realize is that they had served him out of fear. Now they were bonded together with something more powerful than fear.

There was more Stryker didn't know. After the Warrior Monks couldn't find anyone on the Islands, Sawdi had abandoned his plans to chase Stryker and headed back to Edes and Aaron's Palace.

Stryker didn't know that everyone had survived. Stryker didn't know that some of the rebels were rushing to the Continent of Turva. They planned to find the last third of the pendant and destroy it before Stryker. Once they destroyed that piece, the pendant, and Stryker, would be powerless.

Falcon prayed that it would work. And he prayed for something more. He prayed that the curse that Sawdi had placed on him could somehow be lifted. He didn't care how, just that it would be.

THREE

While the Soleis traveled as slowly as possible, the Eos was moving as quickly as it could. So fast sometimes, Meg wished that it would slow down. Like Stryker, she didn't like ships either, and for many of the same reasons.

Mostly, she hated the rocking and rolling. No matter what she did, she constantly felt sick. Everyone tried to help. But nothing they suggested worked for her. Finally, after watching Meg suffer and grow weaker each day, Tarek gave her permission to transform into a raven and fly along with them. Sometimes Wren and Silke joined her, and watching them circle and swoop above the ship made everyone feel better.

It felt so glorious that Meg almost didn't care that turning into a raven was the only thing she could shapeshift into now. And at night, and in the dark, she couldn't do anything at all. She was no longer the shapeshifter that she had once been.

Now she wasn't sure what she was. But at least it seemed as if she was useful. Although she had been told what happened on Lopel, she had no memory of it.

The last thing she remembered was standing with the rest of the rebels, supporting the Mages. They were cloaking every person on the Islands to hide them from the Warrior Monks and Sawdi. The next thing she knew, she found herself lying on a cot in the main room, covered in blankets, and surrounded by her friends.

The story they told was hard to believe. She had been enveloped in fire. Karn pushed her into the circle of Mages. Then a beam of light shot out from her into the sky, turning the Warrior Monks away.

The whole story sounded made up to Meg. But because everyone had confirmed it, she knew it must be true. But why and how was still a mystery to her. However, it didn't appear to be a mystery to Silke or Wren, but they wouldn't talk about it. They would only say all would be revealed in time.

Once Tarek had relented and let her fly during the day, Meg's sickness passed, and she could enjoy the food with the rest of the crew. Captain Lira had put Leon and his men to work cooking for the crew and the passengers.

If they hadn't been speeding towards Turva to stop Stryker, they could have probably enjoyed it more. But even though Raven had told Karn that the Soleis was far behind them, they still worried.

Besides trying to beat Stryker to the pendant, they had to worry about Aaron and Sawdi. Eventually, Sawdi and his Warrior Monks would come after Stryker again, and since they were all heading to the same place, they would once again be battling Sawdi.

No one thought that they could fool Sawdi twice with the same trick. They couldn't do it anyway. There were too many people on the continent of Turva to cloak. Besides, they didn't want to make Sawdi suspicious of what they had done on the Islands so that he returned to them. As far as the three men who ran Aaron-Lem were concerned, there was no one left on the Islands.

Of course, sooner or later, they would try to find out where the people had gone, but the rebels planned on stopping the three tyrants long before they turned their sights back to the Islands.

Meg surprised herself when she realized that she felt homesick for the Islands. She hadn't been there long, and the time had been filled with turmoil. But there was something about them that she loved. They had left friends on the Islands to protect it, and to help the people recover from their conversion from Aaron-Lem. She missed them too, especially Ruth and Roar.

The fact that Ibris and Dax would be leading the healing of the people seemed impossible. It wasn't as hard to believe about Ibris. He had been betraying Aaron all along, just in his own way.

What was harder to believe was that Dax, the man who loved to fight, and had done so much to destroy Mages and Shapeshifters—had betrayed Stryker and Aaron. Now that was surprising. Without Dax's help, they wouldn't have survived. He had turned from being the man who persecuted them to a man determined to protect them.

Meg knew about transformation. She used to be only for herself, caring for no one. All she had cared about was her freedom. But the Islands and the people she met there had changed her. Perhaps that was what happened to Dax.

The revelation that Ibris was not only a wizard, like Tarek, but also his cousin, had shifted something in Tarek. Up until then, he had not allowed himself to believe it possible that his and Leon's family survived the violent takeover by Aaron-Lem.

Now he and Leon had learned that they were not as alone as they had once thought. First, he learned that Dax was his cousin. Along with Ibris. He had learned that his father, Udore, had two brothers. Ian was Ibris' father, and Jori was Dax's. As far as Tarek knew, those two brothers and their families had died, leaving only Dax and Ibris, and they had ended up in Stryker's training camp for boys.

How strange, Meg thought, that the two cousins Tarek didn't know he had, ended up on the Islands together.

As for Leon's family, no one knew how many of them had escaped to the Sanctuary. Meg was glad that Tarek and Leon had more hope now than they did before. It was another reason they were heading to Turva. If their families were still alive, they would be in the Sanctuary, hidden deep within the mountains on Turva near the town of Yeal Thalor.

But Meg knew that checking on them would have to wait. First, they had to find the pendant before Stryker did. Then they had to stop Stryker, Aaron, Sawdi, and the Warrior Monks forever.

Meg laughed to herself. Sure. So easy. No, it was so hard to do that the idea that they could was almost comical. There were so few of them.

But surprisingly, it was Karn who kept assuring them that it was possible. He had been planning this rebellion for a long time. Or so he said. They would have to trust him. So far, he had proved himself. Even Wren seemed to be trusting her wayward husband more these days.

Obviously, Falcon did. He had arrived a few days before to tell them that the Soleis was a few weeks behind them. Without Karn and Falcon's planning, they wouldn't have had the ships ready.

How Karn had known they would need the extra ship, Meg didn't know. But she was glad that he did. Still, Wren said that Karn always had secrets.

Meg hoped that Karn's secrets were for their benefit. How did he know what to do when the fire surrounded her? Secrets. She used to keep them. Now she wanted everything out in the open. It seemed safer that way.

FOUR

S awdi sat on the edge of the cliff while Bolong stood guard. He had temporarily returned the Warrior Monks to the canyon that lay beneath him. He had to think about his next steps, and having to continually control that writhing mass of white dead souls was tiring.

Not so much physically tiring as mentally draining. The ring provided him with energy, but it didn't provide him with enough energy to deal with all that was going on inside his head.

Yes, he loved bringing fear into the world. He always had, long before he found the ring—or the ring found him. But sometimes he felt as if he couldn't be himself anymore. Instead, he was at the mercy of the ring. These thoughts bothered him. He should be able to enjoy the power that he had. He could see the threads of energy that ran the world and manipulate them as desired. Who else could do that? Only him.

The problem lay in that he could only manipulate them when the ring let him or wanted him to. That's what bothered him the most. The ring seemed to be more and more in control every day.

Before the ring, he had enjoyed his freedom to torture who he wanted, and when he felt like it. Plus, he had his own magical skills. They would have been enough to keep him happy forever.

After all, look at what he did to Bolong and his friends. He had turned them into dragons. And that other boy, he had turned him into a Falcon and given him to Stryker. He did that without the ring. He terrorized on his own schedule. Now he was on the ring's schedule.

For some reason, the ring was letting him alone at the moment, and he wished he could return to his cabin in the mountains. But that wasn't possible. There was the problem of Stryker. Yes, he had let him go. Why not? He was easy to follow, and since he was all by himself, he wasn't all that dangerous.

But why was he heading to Turva? What was there? Falcon wouldn't tell him. Claimed that he didn't know. All he could get out of the ziffering bird was that Stryker was by himself, and heading to Turva. There had to be a reason. Sawdi didn't think it was because Stryker wanted to get away from it all.

It was probably for the same reason that he had gone to the Islands: to get that ridiculous pendant. Of course, Sawdi knew about the pendant and the map that was leading Stryker around by the nose.

He had known about the map, and the pendant, since the three of them were in school together. Sawdi sighed. It was the stupidity of the two men who were supposed to rule the world with their fake religion that was making him tired, and angry.

Why did he have to put up with them? Maybe it was time to kill them both. But what then? Would he let Thamon return to its gods, and return to his cabin in the mountains? Or would he take over Aaron-Lem himself? Become a rich man? That didn't appeal to him at all.

What Sawdi knew for sure was it didn't actually matter what he wanted, it was what the ring wanted that he would have to do.

And when he wasn't so tired, he knew that he couldn't live without creating terror. It was what fed him. Yes, he could stay in the cabin alone for a long time, but eventually, he would have to come out to feed on the terror of the people.

He couldn't blame that urge on the ring. It had been there forever. What he could blame on the ring was the timing of everything, and its apparent desire to run his life.

Sawdi stood. He might as well get back to the palace and deal with Aaron and his paranoia. Plus, Aaron told him that he could play with the prisoners if he wanted to. That sounded like an excellent way to spend his time off. There was one in particular that he hadn't seen for many years. He wondered how he was doing.

Aaron said he tried to get him to talk, but he wouldn't. That was because Udore had not met his techniques yet. Besides, Aaron wanted information. Sawdi didn't. He just wanted to feed on Udore's fear. That made it easy.

****

Bolong sighed along with Sawdi, but not for the same reason. The return of the Warrior Monks to the canyon was a huge relief. Bolong knew that it was temporary, but it made it easier for Suzanne to explore the area around Aaron's palace without the fear of running into the Warrior Monks.

When the Monks were free from their canyon container, there was no place that they didn't slink into and stand quietly watching. White wraiths with black holes for eyes, waiting for a signal that only they heard, before destroying whatever or whoever they were looking at.

Now that they were in the canyon, the silence over the desert landscape was absolute. No humming. No howling. The few beings that lived there had disappeared and would only reappear once Sawdi was on his way.

What Bolong feared was that sooner or later, the Warrior Monks would no longer be under Sawdi's control. After watching Sawdi's ring glow and fade into a light-sucking black, Bolong once again wondered if it was the ring that was controlling the wraiths, and possibly controlling Sawdi, too.

He and Suzanne had talked over that possibility many times since she had arrived. Bolong smiled to himself, happy that no one could tell when a dragon smiled.

Suzanne had changed everything. The moment that he had seen her shift from a dragon into a woman, he knew that his life would never be the same. Not because Suzanne had come to help take Thamon back from Aaron-Lem and the men who controlled it, but for him.

Now, he knew that no matter what happened, he had met the person who was meant for him. What he wasn't sure of was if she knew that he was the man, currently a dragon, for her.

Suzanne was all business. Her sister was at risk. The people of Thamon were in danger. That was what was on her mind. Except sometimes Suzanne's looks lasted longer than necessary, and Bolong clung to the hope that she felt the same way that he did.

As Sawdi walked toward him, Bolong prepared himself. They would be returning to the Palace, and Suzanne had given him a task to do as he flew there. Before Suzanne, he had become complacent about what he saw as he flew.

Now he was to memorize every detail. Suzanne was sure that there was more to the palace and its grounds than there appeared to be.

The time he and his friends had been waiting for all these years was upon them. He couldn't be happier. Even Sawdi's lousy mood couldn't dampen his feelings of joy that finally, the rebellion against Aaron-Lem had officially begun.

FIVE

Ibris was sitting on his favorite bench on the beach in Hetale.
But instead of hiding who he was or how he felt, he was fully
visible. Everyone now knew he was the Preacher. No more black
robes. No more not being part of the community. Finally, he was
serving the people the way that a preacher was meant to serve.

And unlike in the past, this time he wasn't alone. Instead, many
of the Islanders were on the beach with him, watching as Etar and
Trin crossed overhead.

When the blue light flashed, he no longer had to hide his silent
whoop of joy. This time, Ibris joined in with the rest of the crowd
as they whooped out loud. The sound brought tears to Ibris' eyes.
It was these seemingly small things that got to him. Things he never
thought he would get to experience again. Yes, Ibris was happy.

It was a good day. It wouldn't have mattered if there had not
been a blue flash. It still would have been a good day. They were
all free from the rule of Stryker and Aaron-Lem. The Mages and
shapeshifters were no longer in hiding. They were part of the
community again, openly joining the people in the Market on the
Arrow.

The cold season had a few weeks to go, which made it early for
a Market, but once the people realized that the Kai-Via was gone,
they needed a place to meet and talk about what had happened.
Samis and his followers were the first to erect tents on the Arrow,
and they invited other people to join them. It took a few days

before the people realized that it was safe to gather. There was no one left to punish them or take a percentage of their earnings or their gold and jewels.

Ruth and Roar ran one of the first booths on the Arrow. But they weren't selling anything. Instead, they were returning all the gold and jewels found hidden in Stryker's room.

Their booth always had a long line of people waiting to identify what was theirs, and then that line would move off to the other booths where they bought food and clothing. It hadn't taken long before the happy chatter that used to be associated with the Market on the Arrow had returned.

Not that the withdrawal of Aaron-Lem had been easy. The drugged water in both the pool and the chalice did not easily leave some of the people's systems. Helping them was something that Oiseon Tod and some of the other Mages were attending to.

The drugging of the pool was something that Ibris hadn't known about, and the fact that Dax had been responsible for it had been a source of more than one heated conversation between them.

On the other hand, Ibris knew he was at fault too. He should have noticed. So many things happened because he hadn't been paying attention, and he could have. Instead, Ibris had chosen to look away, and that act of cowardliness and the resulting feeling of guilt weighed heavily on him.

It was bad enough that the withdrawal off the drug was difficult, but the removal of his words was also hard for many people. So he began to preach again. But this time without any hidden messages. This time his messages were about freedom and the chance to rebuild their lives.

Ibris' words were inspiring and empowering, although sometimes difficult for the people to hear. Ibris reminded them that they were responsible for themselves. But together, they could rebuild their community. Freedom and community was Ibris' message.

It worked for most of the inhabitants. But not all. Some wondered whose side Ibris was actually on. Despite hearing how Ibris, Dax, and the Mages had protected the Islands, they were not sure of Ibris' and Dax's loyalty. There was talk about making the two of them leave the Islands. But the majority wanted them there, so they stayed.

Others missed Ibris' ability to soothe them and tell them what to do and what to think. They wanted to go back to not thinking. They missed Aaron-Lem.

There were still pockets of people bowing to Aaron in the east, not believing what they had been told about the three founders. Yes, not thinking was often the easier way, but Ibris couldn't be part of that. He couldn't and wouldn't stop it either. They had a right to choose.

Besides, it was the early days. Only a few weeks had gone by. Ibris hoped that over time more of them would realize that freedom was better than not thinking.

When he wasn't preaching, or meeting with the people that used to be called the rebels but now called themselves the Restorers, Ibris walked the Islands and met the people face to face. He wanted to know what they needed, how he could help.

Sometimes he sat in their homes and held their hands and wept with them as they mourned the ones that had been lost. He never asked Dax to come with him. Dax had been responsible for so much of their suffering that it was not a good idea to have Dax be visible in the population. It was dangerous for him and distressing for the people.

Instead, Dax had moved into a vacant home on Hetale, and Ibris visited him as often as he could. Like many of the people on the Islands, Dax was having a hard time adjusting.

Dax was used to fighting and manipulating people. What could he do now? Ibris and Dax were in the process of figuring it out. In the meantime, Dax moped around the house, and Ibris worried about him. Not just because he didn't seem to have any energy, but because Ibris wasn't completely sold on Dax's reformation.

Yes, Dax had helped save the Islands. Yes, Dax had betrayed Stryker. But Ibris couldn't help thinking that perhaps all that was part of a bigger plan that perhaps Dax was deciding whether or not to put into play. Ibris hoped he was wrong. They were cousins, old friends, but they were former enemies too. Which one would Dax choose this time?

All Ibris could do was continue to meet with him, and this time pay attention. He could never look away again.

As Ibris walked through the Market on his way to visit the people of Woald on Lopel, his thoughts turned to his other cousins, Tarek and Leon. They were on their way to Turva. He hoped that they were doing well.

One thing that Ibris and the Restorers had agreed on was not to tell the people that Ibris was a wizard.

That skill was something he had hidden his entire life, so keeping it hidden longer was natural, and he assured himself that it was for the people's protection.

If necessary, he could use it. Otherwise, he wanted the Islanders to find their own strength. He would not always be there.

Once the Islands had settled in, he wanted to go in search of what happened to his family. He had always believed that they had all died. But what if that wasn't true?

Six

K arn watched Wren as she and Meg wove their way through the masts and into the clear blue sky. They were flying as if they didn't have a care in the world.

He smiled to himself, wishing that it were true. Wishing that they weren't on a mission that was far from over, and could cost some of them their lives. But Karn had made himself a promise that he would not let anything happen to Wren. If someone had to die, it would be him.

All the plans he had put into place the last few years were starting to unfold. But sometimes he wasn't sure if he had made it too complicated, and that everything he had done would crumble into nothingness. All his work, and plans, and ideas would be worthless. Sometimes it was hard to keep the tangle of threads that he was pulling straight in his mind.

But proving to Wren that he loved her, and she could trust him, would make it all worthwhile.

Still, Karn was beginning to think that it would be better if someone other than himself also knew what he had done. Because if something happened to him, no one would understand what was happening, and it would all be for nothing, and people's lives would be lost.

However, if he told what he had done would they believe him, or would they think he had betrayed them, and not let the plans continue?

He was afraid to tell Wren. She knew him too well. She knew about his recklessness and rash decisions. It would be too easy for her to assume he was doing it again, and she would be unwilling to put her friends' lives in danger on the off-chance that he was doing the right thing.

Karn dropped his head into his hands and sighed, still not clear about what to do. A few seconds later, he felt a light breeze ruffle his hair. He looked up to see Silke hovering in front of him. An Okan. He had never met one before Silke, but he had heard about them. There weren't that many left on Thamon. They were a race that was always in service to a wizard, staying with a lineage for many generations.

Although she had what Karn thought was a ridiculous name, Silke Featherpuff was the perfect description for the Okan that had chosen Tarek's grandfather, father, and now Tarek.

Her hair looked like feathers, but the rest of her looked like a china doll, shaped more like a bird. During the day, it was hard to see that she also lit up and was always blinking on and off. How slow or fast seemed to depend on how she was feeling.

Right now, Karn could see that it was a slow, steady pulse. But as she hovered in front of his face, it was evident that she had something on her mind. They stared at each other for a few seconds until Silke said, "You have to tell someone."

Karn didn't try to deflect what she said or pretend that he didn't understand. The little that he had seen, he knew that Silke was aware of much more than the rest of them. How she knew things, he didn't know.

The answer wasn't any more evident than how Silke flew. She might have had feathers for hair, but they weren't helping her fly.

Silke could also shapeshift to a spider or transport herself in a blink of an eye. But those were what she considered "tricks," and she only did them if it was necessary. Sure, she might have read his thoughts, but even that would have been difficult. He had learned long ago how to hide his thinking, keeping the doors to his mind carefully locked.

So instead of asking how, or what she knew, Karn simply asked, "What do you suggest?"

"Oh, you are too smart to be asking this question. You already know you need to tell Tarek the whole story. Don't leave pieces out. Someone other than you needs to know what you have put into place."

When Karn looked away, she added, "And you best tell him about what has happened to your shapeshifter abilities. He hasn't asked because he is waiting for you to come forward. If you are going to trust someone, trust him."

Before Karn had a chance to reply, Silke had darted away. Across the deck, Tarek was leaning against the rail doing the same thing as Karn had been doing, watching Meg and Wren flying together.

Karn knew that Wren usually didn't trust wizards, having a belief that they never stayed around. But there was nothing about Tarek that suggested that he would leave, and for some reason, Wren seemed to trust Tarek completely.

A small smile was on Tarek's face watching the two women. Karn smiled to himself. Yes, they had that in common. He loved Wren with all his heart, and obviously Tarek loved Meg in the same way. Karn wondered if Tarek knew it, or admitted it to himself.

Tarek glanced over at Karn and smiled. Karn tilted his head towards the stairs that led down into the cabins below deck.

Silke was right. He needed to share what he had done. The fact that Silke apparently already knew and hadn't had him tied up and thrown overboard, gave him hope that he would be believed and that he had done the right thing. But what Karn had to tell Tarek was going to disrupt his entire world.

SEVEN

S ilke followed the two men below deck and into the cabin that Karn shared with four of Leon's men. Karn would have liked to be sharing a cabin with his wife, but Wren wasn't ready to act married again and was staying in a cabin with Meg and Silke.

Not that Silke took up much room, and usually, she remained with Tarek. But Tarek was bunking with Leon, Joseph, and Fionn. "Too much male energy," she said when asked why she wasn't staying with him.

Like all the cabins, Karn's cabin had a small table and chairs in the middle of the room. Two bunk beds lined two of the walls. One wall had a porthole, and the door was on the fourth wall.

Leon's men were used to tight quarters and kept the space neat and well cared for, and Karn had learned to do the same. He figured it was good training for when Wren chose to have him back in her life at night. If she ever did, he would be ready. Karn sighed, thinking about it.

Tarek and Karn moved to the table while Silke stayed on Tarek's shoulder, both waiting patiently for what Karn had to tell them.

Karn stared at them, suddenly more frightened than he had ever been. What would Tarek do when Karn told him what he knew? Where should he start?

"Start at the beginning, Karn," Tarek said, anticipating the problem.

Karn sighed, "Well, you know some of the beginning, so I'll skip the details of being a boy in Stryker's training camp along with Ibris and Dax. You know that Wren helped me escape, and Ibris and Dax looked the other way.

"But there were more boys there that I became friends with before I left. And then, unknown to Wren, I continued those friendships after I escaped. Long after.

"I kept disappointing Wren by not staying around. What I hadn't told her was where I was going and what I was doing. So after feeling abandoned by me one too many times, she gave up.

"I let her think that I was cheating on her so that she wouldn't try to get involved with what I was doing. It seemed safer that way."

Silke shook her head at Karn. "Dumb," was all she said.

"Yes. Dumb. I let Wren go to keep her safe, and then what does she do? Heads straight into danger, rescuing as many Mages and shapeshifters as possible without any concern for herself. Which I submit is why I didn't tell her what I was doing. She would not have had any concern for herself, and what I did was crazy."

Silke and Tarek waited for Karn to go on. Finally, when he seemed to need prodding, Silke said, "So what zonking stupid thing did you do?"

Karn looked up at Silke and smiled. "Well, it didn't seem all that stupid at first, and I still would do it again. But it took me down a few paths I hadn't intended to go.

"It goes back to being in Stryker's training camp. Stryker liked me. He thought he could train me to be a preacher, but I wasn't good at that, so Stryker left me alone most of the time while he figured out what to do with me because he didn't see me as a warrior either."

"No. You are a spy," Silke said.

"I am a spy. You're right. I saw so many things people did not want me to see, and I was at least smart enough to keep quiet. And smart enough to know that what I saw would lead to trouble for Thamon.

"Sawdi scared me the most. I know most people think that Stryker and Aaron are the rulers of Thamon, but as you know, they are both overshadowed by Sawdi.

"I watched him turn six of my friends into something else. Five of them are the dragons that Sawdi keeps as his own personal crown while demanding that all other dragons be eliminated from the planet.

"Bolong is the head of that crown and is the dragon that Sawdi rides. Bolong and I were close, and I was shocked to see what Sawdi did. At the time, I thought that he would turn them back to boys when he was done messing around with them, but as you know, he never did. I didn't know the other four boys well.

"Then I saw him do it again. As usual, I was hiding when I saw Sawdi change another boy into a falcon. Later that day, I saw him "gift" the falcon to Stryker. I know that Stryker calls him Falcon and Falcon still serves Stryker.

"And, that's the falcon that we all saw with Stryker on the Islands?"

Karn nodded, yes. "Even after Wren and I were married, I couldn't stop thinking about those six boys. Or Sawdi.

"Aaron and Stryker were starting their conversion of Thamon, and after having seen all that I had, I realized that I couldn't sit back and let it happen.

"So I went looking for those six boys. First, I found Falcon. He recognized me, and since he could mind-speak, we made a plan."

Tarek started to speak, and Karn raised a hand to stop him. "Yes, I will tell you about the plan. But first, let me give you the big picture, and what I found at the Palace. I promise I won't keep anything back and will tell you as needed. But there is something I need to tell you first, and that came after meeting with Falcon."

Silke tilted her head, and Karn knew what she wanted to know.

"Yes, Falcon and I communicated together while I was on the Islands. He is on our side. He is betraying Stryker and Sawdi. But it is dangerous for him, so the fewer people that know about it, the safer it will be for him."

Both Tarek and Silke nodded in agreement, but Karn could see that Tarek was still not sure. When he told him the rest of the story, who knew what he would think or do? That's what scared him.

Eight

Tarek stood up and started pacing, leaving Silke sitting on the table, staring at Karn. The two of them stared at each other until Karn softly asked, "Do you already know what I have to tell him?"

Silke waited for a beat before shaking her head, no. "You are quite skilled at concealing your thoughts. I suppose that is how you have survived this long, being a spy and all."

"Are you mocking me?" Karn asked, reverting to his habitual sneer.

"I suppose you developed that face to look threatening?" Silke shot back.

The two of them continued to stare at each other until both of them starting laughing, bringing Tarek's attention back to the table.

"What are you two laughing about?" Tarek asked, looking at them with a puzzled expression on his face. He hadn't seen Silke laugh like that for a while. What could they have said to each other?

"I think what you'll have to accept, dear Tarek," Silke said, "is that Karn is quite good at being a spy and that despite the veneer of smart-ass that he puts on, he is actually quite a softy."

When Tarek and Karn looked at her as if she was crazy, she added, "On the inside, of course. On the outside, he really is a smart-ass.

"But putting all of that aside, to answer your question Karn, no, I don't know what you have done or what you are planning. You have guarded yourself well, and I understand why. What I can see is your distress and worry at what you are going to tell us. The best thing to do is get it over with and let us deal with it.

"You were saying that Falcon and the crown of dragons lead by Bolong are boys, now men, that Sawdi shifted and then locked them into that form?"

At Karn's nod of, yes, she continued, "So, you made plans with Falcon. I assume part of that plan was to have the ship waiting for Stryker, so his escape would lead Sawdi away from the Islands. Is that also why we haven't seen that ship?"

"Yes, the captain of the Soleis and Falcon are keeping the ship moving as slow as possible to give us a chance to get to Turva before Stryker does.

"Falcon sees the map when Stryker opens it, and he has told me where the map is leading them, which is one reason why I needed to tell you about Falcon. If you want to land closest to the pendant, I know where that would be because of him. Not because of magic. I am only a spy."

"And a dragon," Silke said.

When Karn didn't move, Silke tilted her head in thought. "If you are a dragon, why haven't we seen you do that? We are out to sea. You could fly with Wren and Meg."

When Karn didn't answer, she said, "Wait. You can't shift into a dragon, can you?"

Karn shook his head, no.

"Have you lost your abilities to shapeshift the same as Meg has?" Tarek asked.

"I didn't lose them. I traded them. That one moment of being a dragon was the last of it. I needed that part to get to the Islands." Karn said.

"You traded them?" Silke blurted. "How could you? And for what?"

Unconsciously Karn reached up and touched his left shoulder, causing his shirt to move away enough for Silke to see what was underneath it.

"Is that part of the story? That scar?" she demanded.

"Yes," Karn sighed. "But it will take some telling to get to that part, and I think perhaps I should tell everyone all at once."

Tarek nodded and left the room, leaving Silke and Karn alone staring at each other again.

"You asked for the others for him, didn't you?"

Karn nodded, "I thought he should have others around him because what I have to say will change everything for Tarek."

"Again," Silke said, dropping her head.

"Again," Karn agreed.

****

To Karn, it felt as if Tarek was gone for hours, but in reality, it was only a few minutes.

Karn's mind raced, filled with questions that he didn't have the answers for. He worried about the outcome of what he had to say.

Everyone would be affected. But most of all, what would Wren think? Had he done the right thing? Was he doing the right thing now? Should he tell everything, or leave out part of it for now?

By the time everyone filed into a cabin built to hold four people, it was packed and stuffy. But whatever Karn was going to tell them was not something they wanted the crew to hear. Even though they assumed that everyone on the Eos was on their side, Karn had proven that spies could be anywhere or anything.

They had to take Karn's word that Falcon was on their side and that Karn was telling the truth about everything else. They had to start somewhere, and that somewhere was what Karn had to say to them.

31

After everyone settled down, Silke took the stage and encapsulated everything Karn had told them into a few sentences.

She finished by telling them that, yes, there were many unanswered questions, but they would have to wait for the answers. Instead, it was time to hear the rest of what Karn had to tell them because it could impact where they were going and what they planned to do.

After Silke finished speaking, she nodded at Karn for him to begin.

Taking a deep breath, Karn plunged ahead. "I went looking for Bolong and the other four dragons."

That's as far as he got before Wren lifted her hand, "Which means you went to the Palace?"

"Which means I went to the Palace. Which is where I have been all this time until I came to the Islands."

No one said anything. If Karn had expected everyone to start talking, either because they were mad at him, or curious, he was wrong. Instead, he was met with stony silence.

Finally, Wren asked, "So you worked for Aaron?"

Karn nodded, "But not the way or for the reason that you think."

It was Silke who asked, "As a spy."

"As a spy," Karn affirmed.

NINE

Across the sea, on the continent of Edes, Aaron woke up in his Palace one morning and realized that the white wraith that had been following him around was gone. He breathed a sigh of relief. Maybe Sawdi had destroyed the Warrior Monks, and they would never return.

But he knew that wouldn't be true. It was wishful thinking. What he wished is that he had never asked Sawdi to return. Wished that Sawdi hadn't raised those people from the dead and then turned them into what they had stupidly called Warrior Monks.

At the time, it had seemed like a good idea. It was a scary name. It made the three of them laugh as they dreamed up ways to control Thamon together using a religion they invented.

That was when he, Stryker, and Sawdi were friends. Or at least as good friends as men could be that wanted to rule the world. What he and Stryker had not realized was that they would have no power over the Warrior Monks. They belonged to Sawdi and only Sawdi.

Too late Aaron had begun to realize that Sawdi might have been in charge the whole time, leading him and Stryker into situations that only Sawdi could control.

Sawdi had them fooled with that quiet voice of his, and then that idiotic desire to live alone on a mountain. Who would choose to disappear like that if they wanted to rule the world? To Aaron, this was not how it was done.

Being a ruler of a world would look more like what he was doing. Live in a palace embedded and embellished with gold and jewels collected from all his people all over the planet Thamon. It would look like having people who served only him. Like his Blessed Ones. People willing to be blinded so they could be in his presence, the God that they worshiped.

Aaron sighed. Sawdi didn't seem to want any of those things. No jewels, no servants, not even one of the women of the Blessed Ones. Sawdi had turned it all down.

Instead, even in the Palace he preferred a room with only a bed, a table, and a window. A plain one. As plain as possible.

All of which made it impossible for Aaron to find ways to distract Sawdi from his plans. Whatever they were. Even though Aaron had barely seen Sawdi since he had returned from the Islands, he felt his influence and presence all the time.

Aaron was always waiting for the other shoe to drop. What was going to happen next? How terrible would it be?

Sawdi had come to see Aaron after returning and given him the briefest of reports. Somehow all the people of the Islands had escaped. The Warrior Monks had swept through every home, every cave, forest, and beach and found no people who lived there.

When Aaron asked Sawdi how that could have happened, Sawdi snapped his fingers, and the Warrior Monk that had lived in the corner of his throne room started to vibrate. Aaron got the message. Don't ask questions. Just listen.

Aaron said that it didn't matter that they weren't there. It was just a bunch of Islanders, newly converted, not valuable to him. He had gone to get Stryker, and Stryker had escaped, so Sawdi returned to the Palace to plan what to do next.

All of it confused Aaron. Why had Sawdi put the Warrior Monks away? Yes, he was grateful that they were gone, at least for now, but why or where were they? Wasn't Sawdi going to continue looking for Stryker?

Was it true that Stryker was betraying the two of them, or was he running because he knew that Sawdi was coming after him? Where was Stryker going? Why didn't Sawdi seem to care?

And what about Ibris and Dax? Did Stryker take the two of them with him? Stryker said they weren't on the Islands. The only people he found were the remaining six Kai-Via. Since Sawdi didn't bring them back with him, Aaron assumed that they died by Sawdi's hand.

What bothered Aaron the most was why Sawdi was not chasing Stryker. What was he waiting for? Aaron could barely admit it to himself, but he wanted Sawdi to go after Stryker.

One of them would kill the other. That would leave him with one less person to get rid of when he took over all of Aaron-Lem, which is what had to happen. After all, the religion was named after him. It was his. His to control. His to take whatever he wanted when he wanted to have it.

Which reminded him. What happened to all the gold and jewels that were on the Islands that Stryker had collected? Did Stryker have time to send them to him, or were they still on the Islands? Why didn't Sawdi bring them back with him?

Truthfully, he knew the answer to that question. Even if Sawdi knew where they were, he wouldn't tell him. Sawdi liked tormenting Aaron. Sawdi knew that the loss of what belonged to Aaron would eat at him.

It gave Sawdi pleasure to torture people, which was really the answer to why Aaron was afraid of Sawdi.

Whatever Sawdi was up to would mean torture for someone. And it could just as easily be him as anyone else. And not just the pain of not having what he wanted. There were far worse tortures than that. Aaron should know.

Together, they had all planned many ways to torture people. But he was sure that Sawdi had spent much of his time in his cabin thinking of new ways to inflict pain.

Aaron thought back to when he wasn't terrified of Sawdi and wondered when the relationship had changed.

The memory of tripping over the stone and finding the box with all those goodies came to mind. It seemed to Aaron that the change from powerful bully to a tyrant driven by the desire to cause pain began on that day.

Was it something in the box? He and Stryker had divided what they had found, while Sawdi seemed barely interested. So if it started that day, what caused the change?

He could have been imagining that's what happened, but he didn't think so. It seemed to him that if he found the answer, he would be the most powerful person on Thamon. It was time to ask more of his spies, especially the one he had been training to take Stryker's place.

In the meantime, he still had his secret that no one, not even Sawdi, had discovered.

It was his and his alone. He had thought it up himself, and it was this secret that eventually would make all of Thamon his. Aaron knew that Sawdi thought he was weak and incapable.

But he wasn't.

TEN

T arek did precisely what Karn was afraid he would do. He stormed out of the cabin and into the wheelhouse where Captain Lira was commanding the ship. Tarek grabbed Captain Lira by the neck of his cloak and shouted into his face to change course—immediately.

It wasn't Tarek's words that shocked Lira as much as the yelling. Was a wizard yelling?

"Turn the ship around?" the Captain stuttered.

He couldn't refuse Tarek. Tarek was a wizard, what could he do but obey him?

However, before he could chart the new course and begin the process, Silke appeared in the cabin and held up her hand for him to stop.

Tarek glared at Silke, but Wren and Karn were right behind her, and the two of them dragged Tarek away. Silke stayed behind and asked Captain Lira if he could stop the ship while they decided what to do.

Lira nodded and then called out to his crew to lower the sails, which they did, but not happily. He could hear their grumbling and cursing. He couldn't blame them. He understood. All of his crew were looking forward to returning to Turva. For most of them, Turva was their homeland.

Just recently, they had gained a glimmer of hope that maybe a few members of their family had survived Aaron-Lem's takeover after all.

This voyage had been different than when they had brought Leon and his men to the Islands. On that trip, they had to tiptoe around Stryker, always worried that they would displease him. Stryker was known for tossing men overboard for no other reason than he hadn't liked what they looked like.

Although a few months before, Captain Lira and his men had picked up the Mages from the Islands and taken them to Turva, they had thought that the Mages were only escaping the Islands.

No one had told them that the Mages were going to try and find the people who had moved to safety before the coming of Aaron-Lem. The Mages and Leon's two men, Joseph and Fionn, who had come with them, were exhausted and barely spoke.

After dropping them off at the small harbor at Yeal Thalor, the Eos had returned to the Islands to wait for the rebels.

Now that they were sailing to Turva once again, Leon and Tarek had taken the time to tell the crew why the Mages had wanted to go to Yeal Thalor.

Leon explained that some of the people of Thamon had believed the ancient documents that foretold a time when three men would attempt to take over the planet in the name of a religion that they made up. It had been so long since the foretelling that most people had decided it was a myth.

However, Leon and Tarek explained that there were pockets of people who believed the stories to be true. So when rumors of Aaron-Lem's take over had begun, they had moved to a safe place on Turva. A Sanctuary.

When the crew asked if Leon and Tarek knew who had believed the stories, and if they were still at the Sanctuary, Leon and Tarek had said they didn't know. In fact, when they had returned to their homelands after being at sea and found their villages destroyed, they had believed that everyone had died. So all their thoughts had turned to stopping Aaron-Lem.

It was only after saving the Islands that they had let themselves believe that someone in their family might still be alive. Leon and Tarek knew that their families had believed the prophecies, which made it possible that at least someone had survived.

However, before they could search for possible survivors, they had to find and destroy the pendant before Stryker did.

Because if Stryker found the last part of the necklace, then all they had done so far wouldn't matter. The stories of the pendant—made by Tewao, God of the skies, designed for his son—made the idea of Stryker, or anyone, putting it together again, terrifying.

Tewao had it made to be used to do good. But Tewao had discovered that given too much power, people only wanted more of it.

Why Tewao had not destroyed the pendant instead of breaking it into thirds and then hiding it, no one knew. Perhaps it couldn't be destroyed, but the rebels intended to try.

That's why they were heading for Turva. They knew that Stryker was going there, and the only reason he would be going to Turva was that it was where he believed he would find the missing piece.

But now that they knew about the Sanctuary, the crew wanted to look for members of their family who might have survived. Once they docked on Turva, most of his crew would follow the path of the Mages.

Even though Captain Lira's family did not come from Turva, he understood how his men felt. He had promised not only to take them there, but to wait in the harbor for them to return.

It hadn't been a hard decision to make. This crew was like family to him. Without this crew sailing with him, Lira had no desire to return to the sea. He would wait and see who wanted to sail with him after this was all over.

It sometimes surprised Captain Lira when he realized that he had become a rebel. Perhaps more passive than the ones he was transporting to Turva, but a rebel. If anyone ever discovered what he and his crew had been doing, they would all be killed by one of Stryker's spies.

So Lira understood why the men were unhappy about pausing in the middle of the ocean. But there was nothing he could do. He would have to wait until someone told him what happened to make Tarek behave in this way.

He would have to wait until someone told him where they were going. If they weren't going to Turva, where would they be going?

Below deck, that was the question everyone was asking. Where were they going? Were they going to Turva for the pendant or to Aaron's Palace on Edes?

Eleven

Meg was having trouble staying in the cabin. Tarek was withdrawn and angry. Everyone was silent, not sure what to say. Besides, even though the Eos was not moving, the waves were rocking the ship, and the only good thing about the packed room was there was no room to fall over. But the air was heavy and stale, and she longed for the breeze on her face.

She glared at Karn. It was all his fault. If he had never shown up or at least kept his mouth shut, they would be happily sailing towards Turva. Temporarily safe from Aaron, Stryker, and Sawdi's Warrior Monks.

But she knew she was fooling herself. They were never safe while those three men controlled Thamon. And Karn had come to save them at his own expense, willing to sacrifice his freedom and his abilities to bring them information that may, in the end, stop Aaron-Lem. Maybe. But it did appear that Karn was sincere in his desire to be on their side.

Anyone could see his love for Wren was real. There was no way he would be doing anything to jeopardize that relationship. He had done everything he had for her.

Looking at his downcast face, Meg realized that everyone was mad at Karn because he was a messenger. Surprisingly he was not only a messenger of bad news but of good news. And it was the good news that had made Tarek mad.

Did that make sense? Meg asked herself. She wondered if she would ever understand how other people thought. Her own transformation from a shapeshifter to something else had been traumatic.

No, not had been. Still was. And then standing in the fire and then a beam of light, well, what was she? She didn't know, and neither did anyone else. Or at least they weren't telling her.

The one thing Meg did know is that she felt something profound for Tarek, and she wanted to take away his pain because that was what was causing the anger. Pain.

How she knew that she wasn't sure, but when Meg looked over at Silke and received a nod from her, Meg knew she was right.

It was Wren who took over. What was happening wasn't easy for her, either. All this time, Wren had tried to forget Karn, thinking he had betrayed her, abandoned her, and all along he had been living in Aaron's castle. Not as part of Aaron's team, but as a servant. A Blessed One.

His tale had been gruesome. He described how they lived, how Sawdi stuck knives into Blessed Ones to make sure that they were blind, how he had let it happen, not flinching as the blade came towards him, knowing that it was the only way to remain in Aaron's service.

He described how Aaron used something that sent out a beam of light that disintegrated everyone that displeased him. How often he had seen it done, and not flinched at the sight.

How hard Karn had to work to look blind and watch what Aaron was doing. The tears he wanted to shed as he swept up the ashes of his friends.

And finally, how he decided that it was time to escape and how Falcon had helped him. Helped him all along by keeping him up to date as much as possible about how Aaron was feeling so he could stay out of his way.

But it was finding out how Karn had managed to appear blind, and how he had survived as a Blessed One that had turned Tarek from a gentle wizard into an angry man.

Wren had asked that question that changed everything. "How did you lose your powers, Karn? What did you trade for them?"

"I traded them for the ability to look blind so that I could pass as a Blessed One. It wasn't a trade so much as an exchange. And I would do it again in a second. Being a dragon was wonderful. But it wouldn't have done any good inside of Aaron's Palace."

"Who did that for you?" Wren had asked, not realizing that the answer would change everything.

Karn had turned to Tarek, and with pain in his eyes, answered, "Your father, Udore, did, Tarek."

Tarek had paused and then asked, "You knew my father? He did this before you went to the Palace? I don't understand how that could have happened. How would either of you have known about the Blessed Ones before Aaron-Lem came to Turva?

"In fact, even then, how would he have known? I don't think any of us knew about the Blessed Ones. It sounds horrible, but how did he know?"

"I didn't know your father, then," Karn replied. "I met him later at the Palace. I found him there. In prison."

With those words, the entire room had gone silent, and then Tarek exploded. "My father is alive? In prison? On Edes? Is he still there? How is he?"

Without waiting for an answer, he had stormed out of the cabin up to see Captain Lira.

Now they were back in the cabin, and those questions needed to be answered. Then they could decide where to go. To Turva for the pendant, or to Edes to rescue Tarek's father.

Karn waited for Wren to ask the question of him that would help them make that decision. He would answer all of those truthfully, but there was still one piece of information he wondered if he should tell.

As he waited for Wren to speak, Karn glanced over at Silke, who nodded. Did she mean that he should tell everything, or keep that part a secret for now?

And how did she know there was more? For the hundredth time since he met her, Karn wondered who Silke really was, and what did she know?

Opening his thought more to Silke, he waited for a more precise answer. Then he heard her say, "Tell it all."

Karn sighed. He knew she was right. But it wouldn't be easy, and he did not know what could be done about it.

TWELVE

U dore sighed. It was time. He had waited many years for this moment. Perhaps he shouldn't have waited. Maybe, if he had acted sooner, he could have stopped Aaron, Stryker, and Sawdi from doing what they had done.

But as much as Udore wished he would have done something, he knew that he couldn't have. It wouldn't have made any difference, anyway. Instead, he had done what he could while allowing Aaron to lock him away in a cell for all these years. But finally, the time had come. Everything was in place.

Of course, many things could go wrong. But they had to start somewhere. Udore hoped that everyone was ready. All this time he had placed all his trust in the two boys from Stryker's training camp. There was no reason to stop trusting now.

The day Karn appeared in his cell and asked Udore to take away all his skills except one, Udore had said no. It was a horrible trade, and he didn't want to do it. But Karn was persuasive.

Yes, Karn had argued, Udore could walk away from the Palace anytime he wanted to. He was a wizard after all. He could escape, but to do what? However, if Udore stayed and became part of the resistance inside the Palace, they had a chance. Karn claimed that he could find others who would join in the cause, and when the time was right, they would rise.

Karn returned time and again before Udore agreed. The only time anyone came to Udore's cell was to bring rotten food once a day, so they felt relatively safe to plan together. However, they took no chances that someone might be listening, so they would sit quietly in the dark and mind-speak to each other.

Karn argued that if he could become one of the Blessed Ones, he would hear everything that Aaron was planning. Udore was hesitant, afraid for Karn.

Udore had witnessed the destruction of his entire village. Although his family had left months before because they had believed the prophecies, he had stayed behind trying to convince others to go, too.

Finally, he was too late. Stryker's forces arrived and leveled the village, capturing Udore in the process. It was intentional, Udore now knew. Stryker destroyed the town to get to him.

Udore alternated between despair and fury as Karn told Udore how Stryker had destroyed many villages to get to the young boys and girls that he and Aaron wanted.

But the more Karn spoke, the more determined Udore became. If his family was still alive, Karn was right. They would need to be part of a substantial resistance because until they eliminated the three men who formed Aaron-Lem, there would be no safe place in all of Thamon for any of them.

So, eventually, Udore agreed to what Karn wanted. He took Karn's ability to be a shapeshifter away and removed the ability to do any form of magic.

The only thing Udore left for Karn was the ability to transport himself so that they could still talk. It wasn't much, and Karn's transportation abilities had a limited range. But to be able to be seen as one of the Blessed Ones, and to survive the blinding and stabbing, Karn needed all that he once had to protect himself.

The day that Karn convinced him, and Udore took Karn's powers away, Udore waited in fear for Karn to return and tell him that he had survived the blinding. When Karn didn't return,

Udore alternated between tears and raging anger. To Udore's relief, Karn showed up weeks later.

It had worked. But it had taken so much out of Karn that he could not transport until he recovered. But it was worth it. Even when Sawdi showed up for one of his visits and tested Karn by stabbing him, it had been worth it because Karn had been right.

Not only was he privy to many plans for Aaron-Lem, but he was able to find others who would join him in the resistance. One day Falcon arrived in the small garden beside where the Blessed Ones lived, and that changed everything. Although at first Karn didn't believe him.

Karn thought Falcon was a spy for Aaron, checking on the Blessed Ones. Although Falcon was checking on the Blessed Ones, it was not in the way that Karn had thought. Falcon was there to find someone who would be willing to help him stop Aaron. That day, he recognized Karn from Stryker's training camp and mind-spoke to him.

At first, Karn didn't know him. But then Karn remembered watching Sawdi turn one of the boys into a falcon. If this was the same falcon, yes, he knew him. Eventually, they gained each other's trust, and then they expanded their network to the five dragons owned by Sawdi.

All the while, they were planning the future. But Falcon, Udore, and Karn knew that they needed more help.

Udore talked to them about what he knew about the prophecies. From what he had read, Udore believed that the Islands were where the resistance would begin. First, Stryker would head there looking for the pendant, and others would hear the call to be there to stop him.

That was when they set the plan in motion. When everything was ready, Udore would leave his cell for good.

On the day that Falcon returned to tell Udore that his son Tarek and his Okan companion Silke were on the Islands, they all knew the time was near. When the light flashed across Thamon, all those in the resistance knew that the time had come. The prophecy of a light calling everyone to action had come true.

But first, Udore had one more thing to do, and he would need the help of the woman, Suzanne, who was living with the dragons, waiting for the next step of the plan. Once he left the cell, all hell would break loose as Aaron and Sawdi searched for him. They had only one chance to rescue the women and children and get them to safety.

He hoped the message he sent with Falcon arrived in time before Tarek did something that ruined their plans.

Thirteen

Walking across the Arrow to Lopel had always been one of Ibris' favorite things to do. And now that the warm season was returning, the Arrow was filling with the multi-colored tents of the Hetale and Lopel merchants, craftspeople, and farmers with early crops.

But what made it both more enjoyable and harder at the same time was that now everyone knew him. Ibris no longer hid behind the Preacher's cloak.

One day he had stood in the market and revealed that he was the man they knew as the Preacher. They hadn't believed him until he spoke, and then there was a stunned silence. Much to their dismay, the Preacher wasn't some godly being as they had imagined him to be. He was only a man.

Or so they thought. Ibris had still not revealed himself as a wizard. He told himself that it was too soon for them to know, but he knew that it was because he wanted to be part of the people. Not set apart as something special.

After getting over the shock of seeing the man behind the robes, most of the people decided to continue to call him the Preacher.

He accepted it for now. Ibris felt that if he could use his skills to help, he would. So every day, Ibris still preached. Usually informally, wherever people gathered.

But he no longer taught Aaron-Lem doctrines. Ibris concentrated on uniting the people and supporting them as they woke up from the trance that he had helped put them in.

Most of the people seemed to understand and accept what he was telling them, but not all of them. Some of them were angry. Which was why walking among the people was both enjoyable and difficult. When he appeared in public, most of the people were kind. Others were not. He was a visible target for those people who hated what he and Dax had done.

Ibris couldn't blame them. But if he joined them in hating himself, he would be of no help now. He hoped that by continuing to show up and help, that the anger and hatred would die down, although Ibris knew it would never be gone entirely. Too much had been done that hurt the people. Too many people had died. Too many people were missing for the pain ever to go away.

Dax was a different story. He never walked among the people. Again, for a good reason. There would be no kind words for him. It would only be anger and hatred.

Everyone understood that it had been Dax that had carried out all the disappearing and killing. So, walking among the people would be dangerous, not for Dax, but for the people. Dax had not lost his warrior mentality. He had only subdued it. Neither Dax nor Ibris knew if it could ever be completely subdued.

As the head of the Islands' Kai-Via, Dax had been ruthless. He had tortured and killed many of their friends and neighbors. It would take the Islanders a long time to forgive Dax. Maybe never.

Yes, Dax had helped save the Islands. But Ibris still wondered if Dax had done it for his own purpose, or because he wanted the people to be free. This was the question that Ibris continued to ask himself. He wanted it to be true that Dax had transformed. But he wasn't sure if he had been. And he needed to be.

He and Dax had spent many nights talking together. They had relived their days in Stryker's training camp. They spoke of their parents, especially their fathers, both of whom had died at Stryker's hand. There were three Rissanen brothers. Ian was Ibris father, Jori was Dax's, and Udore was Tarek's.

Ibris and Tarek had become wizards. Dax had not. Perhaps that had started his underlying resentment and anger. Then when the oldest brother's son turned up on the Islands to save it, Dax's envy grew.

Dax had long suspected that Ibris was a wizard but had kept it a secret. Partly because it gave him leverage if he needed it with Stryker, and partly out of allegiance to Ibris. They had once been very close. It was hard to turn against him, and that was why he had joined him in saving the Islands. But now, who was he?

Dax felt as if he was two people. A man who wanted to do good and a man who needed to do violence. How could he be both? Ibris said he understood, but how could he? Ibris had always been on the side of good. Although Ibris had done violence thinking that it was the right thing to do, it had gone against his nature, and he would never see it as a solution again.

For Dax, this was naïve. Aaron, Stryker, and Sawdi were still intent on taking over Thamon, which meant that the Mages, wizards, shapeshifters, and Ordinaries who would not conform to Aaron-Lem were still in danger. Who would protect them if not someone who was used to, and good at, killing?

Besides, Dax reminded himself, he had always wanted to be the ruler of Thamon himself and had plans to do that. Plans he had laid aside to help his cousins rescue the Islands. But were those plans no longer what he wanted? Had he stopped thinking about them?

Dax had to admit that he hadn't, and despite all the talking that they did together, he never told Ibris about the pull towards power that he continuously fought.

But Ibris knew anyway. He waited in vain for Dax to talk about it. He loved Dax. But that didn't mean that he trusted him. He couldn't put the Islands at risk.

The Mages and shapeshifters who had stayed on the Islands were still in danger from the faction that wanted things to return to Aaron-Lem. They couldn't see that Sawdi had come to kill them all with his Warrior Monks. All they could see is that they were happier under the tenets of Aaron-Lem.

And even though they were free to continue to practice it, as all people were free to choose the god and the religion they wanted to follow, the radical members wanted it to be as it was before. Both Ibris and Dax worried what Dax would do about them. Would he follow them or help stop them?

At that moment, neither of them knew the answer. But after every talk together, the two of them hugged. It was new for them, and it was the best that they could do for now.

FOURTEEN

"You can't go rescue your father, Tarek," Karn said.

Tarek had calmed down a little. Leon had taken him for a walk on the deck, and when he returned, although he was still ready to turn the ship around, he was more willing to listen to what else Karn had to tell him.

"Why not?" he grunted, but without all the anger he had directed at Karn before.

"There is a plan in place, and you will disrupt it.

"When Falcon comes back, he will be bringing the information about the timing of when it will happen. But even if Falcon never returns, we still can't go back there.

"We have to go to Turva. Yes, it's where Stryker is going to get the last part of the pendant, and we need to get it first. But not only that, it is where the prophecies said we are supposed to go."

"What prophesy?" Meg asked. "I keep hearing about it, but I don't understand who wrote it, or who has read it, or who found it, or what it looks like. Is it a book? What?"

"That's a lot of questions, Meg," Karn laughed, "But all good ones! Actually, Tarek and Leon know many of those answers."

Tarek nodded at Leon to answer the question. He wasn't in the mood to share. Tarek recognized the non-wizard behavior he was displaying, but the news that his father had been in prison in

Aaron's castle all this time was bringing up so many feelings he could barely think straight.

Why didn't he know? Why didn't he feel his father's presence in Thamon? What if Silke would have stayed with his father, instead of coming with him? Would his father have escaped?

Before answering Meg's question, Leon turned to Tarek. "All those questions in your head, Tarek, cannot be answered right now, maybe never. And it's keeping you from being present with us. There is a reason why it went that way. Your father had a plan. You know he did. You've got to trust that."

The best that Tarek could do was say, "You're right."

Leon turned back to the group to answer Meg's question.

"I am not an expert, Meg, but both our families, as you know, have read and followed the prophecies for many, many generations. Yes, it's a book. However, it's not made of paper or written in ink. Actually, no one knows what it is made from. Whatever it is, it appears to be indestructible because it never ages."

"Magic made it?" Meg asked.

"Who knows? What I do know is that how to read it has been part of the training for at least a few members of every family. But even if we couldn't read it, it wouldn't matter too much. The story is always told at family gatherings."

"And that story is?" Meg prompted.

"That someday there would be three men who would want to take over Thamon and use a false religion that divided the people, to do so."

"That's it?" Meg asked.

"Well, there is more, but I don't know what it is. I think that Tarek's father does, and that is why he probably allowed himself to be captured. And it gives me hope that it means that the rest of our families are safe, that they made it to the Sanctuary prepared for this time. And when it's over, we will go find them."

Everyone sat quietly, thinking about what that would mean. Meg thought about her sister Suzanne and hoped that she had made it to the Palace safely. She was the only member of her family that she could ever be reunited with, and it would have to be enough.

Meg turned to Karn, "Since you said we are supposed to go to Turva, you must know more of these prophecies too. Did Udore tell you?"

Karn nodded. "Yes, Udore told me. He told me that the pendant would be found on Turva. He said the pendant, and the map that showed where the pieces are, are part of the prophecy. Udore didn't need a map. He just knew that two of the pieces were on the Islands and the other one on Turva. Actually, not that far from the Sanctuary."

"So whoever wrote the prophecies also made the map, and maybe the pendant? Not some god? That is just a myth?"

This time it was Silke who answered. "Probably. And that's enough discussion about that for now. Karn needs to tell you the rest of what is happening on Edes at the Palace."

Meg narrowed her eyes at Silke, who stared right back at her. She wanted to ask her how she knew so much, and what else did Silke know because obviously, she was keeping things from them. But Silke's stare convinced her to give up that line of questioning for now. She turned back to Karn, who seemed to be having a hard time telling them the next part of what he needed to say.

Wren turned to Karn and whispered something in his ear. He looked at her gratefully and squeezed her hand before continuing.

"There was another prisoner at the Palace that was helping Udore, Falcon, and I. She was captured when Stryker raided villages. We all know that Stryker took the young boys to train them to become part of the Aaron-Lem network. But he also took young girls. And he took them for Aaron."

To Meg's surprise, she burst into tears. She had a terrible thought about why Aaron took the girls, and it struck such pain in her heart she couldn't bear it. But she had to know.

"What happened to those girls?" Meg whispered, afraid to hear the answer.

"They became part of Aaron's private plan. His secret. Or what he thought was his secret. We discovered it because one girl he took became part of our resistance. Udore knew her. Knows her. She's his niece."

Turning to Leon and Tarek, Karn added. "A cousin of yours. Ian's daughter and Ibris' sister, Rose."

FIFTEEN

Depending on who looked back on that day, it was either lucky or unlucky that Aaron stopped Sawdi from visiting Udore in his cell on the same day that the rebel's plan began at the Palace.

Sawdi had just finished returning the Warrior Monks to the depths of the cavern and was looking forward to spending a little time doing something satisfying, like torturing Udore, when Aaron stopped him. He had something he wanted to talk about.

Sawdi had reluctantly followed Aaron to a small room that Aaron called his meditation room. For the next few minutes, he was subjected to listening to Aaron's new plans to get more from the people of Thamon and how he proposed to go about doing it.

What Aaron had to say so infuriated Sawdi that he stormed off, forgetting his original purpose to visit the prisoner.

Aaron, in turn, was so offended by Sawdi's reaction that he retreated to his opulent throne room to think through what had happened.

Neither one of them suspected anything other than the usual stupidity or rudeness of the other. But once they were distracted, Udore used a small amount of magic to keep them so upset with each other that neither one of them paid attention to anything other than their anger and resentment.

Although Udore could have used this skill on them more often, he had saved it for this time. He hadn't wanted either one of them to suspect that someone had manipulated their minds. Udore didn't want them to ever know. He wanted both of them to blame the other. Udore knew that division was one way to destroy.

After all, Aaron-Lem had been using division for years to control the people. Aaron-Lem promoted superiority among some people over others. It was an easy way to let people destroy each other.

As soon as Aaron and Sawdi were distracted, Udore left his cell. He made his way to where Aaron kept the women of the Blessed Ones. Udore had done this before. It was how he knew what was happening with those women and Aaron, and how he had found Rose.

But today was different. Today they planned to move the women to the safe place that the resistance had been preparing for them.

It was another reason why Udore hadn't left his jail cell years before. He and the other rebels on Edes needed time to build the space for the women. It was a place where the women could live comfortably. But more importantly, Udore had woven protection spells over it so tightly that he was sure that no one would be able to penetrate them to see where the women were hiding.

When Thamon was free again, the women could choose where they wanted to live, but for now, the Sanctuary prepared for them was the safest spot. Udore wished they could have done this for them years before.

But it had taken time to find the people who were ready to rebel against Aaron-Lem. Then they needed time to build the Sanctuary. Everything had to be done out of sight of anyone who believed in Aaron-Lem and might report them.

So it had taken much longer than Udore and Falcon had planned. And as the years went by, they had to extend the space because not only did Aaron continue to capture women, but he had plans for them that included children.

So it wasn't just the women they were moving. They were moving all the children. Aaron's children. Aaron's secret plan to reseed the world with his children was not as secret as he had believed. Perhaps no one outside of the Palace knew of it, but the rebels on Edes did, and it infuriated them. More than once, they had wanted to storm the Palace and take the women, but Udore continually preached patience. It wasn't time yet.

Now it was. Everything was in place. As the prophecies had foretold, the Islands had been saved. Not only by the Mages, and his son, and his nephews, but by the woman who stood in fire and light.

However, there was another reason why the women and the children could not return to the world yet. It was because some of the children were almost adults. They would need time away from Aaron and his training. A period of adjustment. Otherwise, the rebels would be doing Aaron's work for him. They would be bringing Aaron's children into the world to preach and rule Thamon under the tenets of Aaron-Lem.

Rose was waiting for Udore at the door. She had been preparing the women for years, assuring them that this day would come, and they were more than ready to go. It was the children who would be difficult. Only the very young were with their mothers. The rest were housed separately. Many of them did not remember their mothers. And the older children were already experts in espousing Aaron-Lem.

Rose's daughter, Iris, lived with the children. But Rose had found a way to visit Iris and explain the truth of what was happening. As a result, Iris had done her best to prepare the children with what was coming. It had been harder to keep that secret. Children talk.

Still, Udore knew it was time, and they had to take the chance that everyone was willing. No one could be left behind.

Behind Udore, the rides for the women and children were waiting for them. Six dragons. The women couldn't see them, having been blinded years before by Aaron. Yes, he called the woman Blessed Ones. But they had not chosen to be that. Aaron had chosen for them. Some of the women were not there. Aaron had sent women to every head of the Kai-Via and the Preachers to use if they wanted them. Those women lived nearby every Temple.

Udore had promised Rose that they would rescue those women too, as soon as they could. They would be part of the freeing of Thamon from Aaron-Lem's rule.

The reason they were rescuing the women and children at the Palace now was Udore was leaving Edes and heading to Turva to help stop Stryker. Udore wanted Sawdi to follow him there.

But timing was everything, and Udore hoped he had timed it right.

Sixteen

Rose helped the women and the children onto the dragons. They weren't going far, but none of the children had seen a dragon before, let alone ridden one. They were terrified.

The women did their best to contain their fear and sandwiched children between them to keep them safe, not paying any attention to whether they were their children or not. The children whose mothers had died, either from lack of care, or Aaron's anger, would be taken care of by the others.

In the Sanctuary, rebel women were waiting for the Blessed Ones and their children. They had volunteered to be responsible for their care and retraining.

However, Udore knew that there was a possibility that some of the older children might cause trouble, so men were staying with them, too. Whenever possible, he wanted whole families to be part of the Sanctuary so that Aaron's offspring could see what families looked like outside of Aaron's rule.

Some of the men had not wanted to stay. They wanted to be part of what they saw as the more significant rebellion, but Udore had explained to them how important their role was—to give these women and children a return to themselves.

Bolong, Suzanne, and the four other dragons remained as still as possible as the women and children climbed aboard. Then Udore used a small binding spell to keep them on as they traveled to the Sanctuary. The children were more afraid and initially noisier than he had thought they would be, so he used additional magic to silence the talking and crying.

It was understandable. It was terrifying. This was a whole new world. The people who had guarded them, who now lay asleep in a deep trance in their rooms, had never told them anything other than that Aaron was their father and the god of the world. Udore couldn't blame the guards either. Everyone was afraid for their lives under the reign of Aaron-Lem.

However, the rebels believed that being alive within the prison of Aaron-Lem's rule was not living. They were willing to risk everything to overthrow Aaron-Lem. Udore was deeply grateful to them and prayed that they would be safe.

Across Edes, other rebels, some of them Preachers and Kai-Via, would be waiting for a sign to begin the overthrow. In the meantime, they trained in secret and waited. Udore had told them what signs to look for. If all went well, it wouldn't be much longer.

Considering all that could have happened, the transport of the women and the children went smoothly. Rose did everything she could to make the relocation as comfortable as possible for her friends.

Like Karn, Rose had lived as if she was blind. Udore had protected her, too. But pretending to be blind had been difficult for her. Rose was not a wizard like her brother, Ibris. Rose's magic was like her mother's, found in the small things. But like Ibris, she did know how to soothe and teach with words, and the women listened as she explained to them that they were safe.

Their job now was to get well and be with the children. All the women wept as they searched through the children to find the ones that they knew were theirs, their instinct taking over.

Some children remained unclaimed, but it didn't take long until they were seated with a family. Only the older children stood apart. Rose and Suzanne—who had transformed back into a woman, shocking the children—watched and worried that the older ones might not ever escape Aaron's influence.

There was one last thing for Rose to do, and it was the hardest thing she had ever done. She had to say goodbye to her daughter, Iris. Iris was still a young girl, having just turned thirteen, but she had her uncle's and mother's gift of words, and that gift was what would be needed at the women's Sanctuary. Besides, as Rose said, what they were going to do was too dangerous for her to be there.

Still, they both wept and had to be pulled apart when it was time to go. Suzanne transformed back into Lady the dragon and took Rose to the cave where Bolong, the other four dragons, Udore, and Falcon waited for them.

Once there, they had to say another goodbye. Only Suzanne would be leaving with Rose and Udore. Sawdi would need his dragons to come after Stryker and Udore.

Even though they knew they might never see each other again, Bolong and Suzanne still promised each other that they would and that they would be safe in the meantime.

The last few weeks with the dragons had been good ones for Suzanne. She felt at home with them, especially Bolong. She and Bolong hoped that maybe one day the spell Sawdi had placed on the dragons and Falcon would be dissolved,

So many maybes, Suzanne thought as she shifted back into Lady, and Udore and Rose climbed on. They were headed to Turva. This time Suzanne would experience flying out of time.

Bolong promised her that it was an experience that she would enjoy, and she trusted Bolong. Besides, she never wanted to make a trip across the ocean again in regular time.

Bolong and his friends wept tears of both joy and sorrow as they watched them leave, but mostly joy. The rebellion had begun in earnest.

There would be a brief moment of peace before someone discovered the missing women and children. They were counting on no one wanting to be the one that reported them missing. Aaron was known for killing messengers. But eventually, someone would tell Sawdi that they were gone, and that Udore was not in his cell.

After Suzanne, Udore, and Rose left, Falcon left to update Karn, grateful that he too could fly out of time. When he returned, they would put the next part of the plan into action.

Falcon couldn't wait until he could reveal his true colors and stop pretending that he was serving Aaron. Even if he had to stay a falcon forever, it was a price he was willing to pay.

SEVENTEEN

I t took one day until all hell broke loose in the Palace. The women and children were well protected in their Sanctuary and were isolated from the aftermath of their disappearance. Aaron had every soldier and citizen who lived around the Palace looking for them.

As the rebels had predicted, although the guards knew immediately that the women and children were gone, aware of what would happen to them if they reported it, they didn't. Instead, they fled. Not one of them stayed behind.

For most of them, it was the opportunity that they had been waiting for, a chance to escape Aaron's cruelty. Others fled because they knew Aaron would turn them to ash if he found them.

It was the faithful Blessed Ones who brought food to the women who eventually told Aaron. For them, they were in service to the one true God, and if he killed them, they deserved it.

At the news, Aaron's screams traveled through the Palace like a knife, awakening Sawdi from a deep sleep. Sawdi knew immediately that something terrible had happened. Not just because Aaron was screaming. Aaron was an idiot and could be screaming over missing gemstones. No, it was because he realized that he had been put to sleep, and there was only one person capable of doing that to him. Udore.

Sawdi slipped on his black cloak as he ran through the halls to the prison, yelling for assistance as he did so, although, in his heart, he knew that it was too late. Seeing the empty cell, the guards gasped in shock. How could this have happened?

Sawdi didn't need to ask the question. But he did blame the guards. Truthfully, he knew he should blame himself. He should have realized that Udore was using his wizard's skills all along, but he and the ring needed to lash out somewhere, so he turned his fury onto the guards.

However, killing them gave him no pleasure. Not that he was looking for pleasure. He was looking for answers. Why had Udore chosen to leave now? Had he had the ability to do it all before? Obviously, the drugs they had been giving him had not worked. As Sawdi strode through the hall to the throne room where he knew he would find Aaron in a frenzy, he asked himself, why now?

When Aaron told him the women were missing, Sawdi knew why.

"What about the children?" Sawdi asked.

Aaron turned even whiter than his usually pale self and choked on his words as he said, "You know about the children?"

Aaron's blatant stupidity and apparent lack of any sense at all was one thing too much for Sawdi. His patience and tolerance of Aaron came to an end and he reached out with the power of the ring and slapped Aaron so hard he flew off the chair and onto the gold floor, where he slid for a few feet. Aaron lay on the floor, staring up at an infuriated Sawdi, and wondering if it was safe to move.

"Get up, you shivering, shrunken, stupid, coward," Sawdi said, keeping his voice tight and controlled as his fury simmered beneath the surface.

Aaron slid back a little further from Sawdi before pushing himself up off the floor. A part of Aaron's brain noticed that his bejeweled robed had chipped the floor as he slid across it. He would have to have it repaired immediately.

Recognizing the stupidity of that thought while the women and children were gone and Sawdi was revealing his true feelings for him, Aaron did his best to be still and face Sawdi, reminding himself that, after all, he was a god.

"All you ever had to do was follow what I told you to do," Sawdi hissed. "I let you have all the extravagance because it helped the people believe in your power. But you have none. That stupid wrist thing you wear makes you look powerful, but if I take it away, you are helpless."

If it were possible, more blood drained out of Aaron's face at Sawdi's words. He knew about the wrist band too? How many people knew?

"More than you think, you stupid man. Dax has one. He used it on the Islands to destroy the prison camp and all those Mages. Maybe someday he'll use it on you. I won't care who wins. Either way, I will be done with at least one of you. But to make it fairer, I think I'll get rid of the rest of them right now."

Sawdi turned to the chest where Aaron kept the bands, lifted his left hand, and pointed his ring at it. A blast of light flared out, and the chest vanished.

"No!" Aaron screamed, looking at the space where the chest had once been. Now he only had one wrist band. How had Dax gotten one? How had Sawdi known about it?

At the enormity of how powerless he felt, Aaron slipped back onto the floor and dropped his head to his knees.

Sawdi waited, vibrating with the rage that he was working hard to control. This was not the time to destroy all that he had built. People still expected Aaron to act like a god. If he wanted the reign of Aaron-Lem to continue, he needed Aaron, at least for now. And he needed him to be seen as a god.

The two Blessed Ones in the room started shivering knowing what was coming.

"I'll leave you to clean up your messes," Sawdi said, nodding toward the two Blessed Ones. "When I get back, I expect you to look and act like a god, or maybe someone else will take your place."

Aaron lifted his eyes to the two Blessed Ones and did what Sawdi had asked him to do. But he remained on the floor staring at the gems on his robe and the chips on his golden floor, and wondered where it had all gone wrong. Aaron didn't need to ask Sawdi where he was going. In the distance, the low hum of the Warrior Monks began, and Aaron knew that soon one would be in the corner watching him again.

For a brief moment, Aaron felt sorry for Udore, wherever he was, because Sawdi was coming after him, and no one would be able to stand against him. How had he never seen that before? Aaron asked himself.

The answer was simple. Sawdi didn't want him to know. And now it was clear why.

EIGHTEEN

S tryker couldn't take it much longer. If the Soleis didn't start
moving faster, he would kill Captain Kosti and take over. No,
he didn't know anything about sailing, but he did know how to
motivate people through punishment.

This trip had been the worst one Stryker had ever taken. Once
he got off the ship, he promised himself that he would never get
on one again, even if it meant he had to stay on Turva forever. He
could build his own palace on Turva, or live on a mountain like
Sawdi and control everyone from there.

It hadn't helped that the ship was always rocking. Had it done
that before? Stryker asked himself. He couldn't see how it was
happening. Sometimes the ship rolled even when the sea was calm.

The crew didn't seem to mind. No one but him appeared to be
constantly ill. It also didn't help that the cook on the Soleis was
utterly incapable. Once again, no one seemed to mind. Not that it
mattered at the moment, since he couldn't eat.

Gathering all his energy, Stryker burst into the Captain's cabin
to tell him to move the Soleis along faster or die, just as Falcon
appeared. "Thank the gods," Stryker said. "Where have you been?"

When Falcon told him that they weren't far from their
destination, Stryker retreated to his seat on the deck where he felt
the least sick and started imagining how it would feel once he
found the final piece of the pendant. He felt for the bottom section

that he kept sewn into a pocket of his robe, and the top part that hung around his neck.

It wouldn't be much longer until all this would be over. The map continued to point him to the same place on Turva. Once he had the pendant, he would be the ruler of all of Thamon.

A frisson of fear ran through Stryker as he thought about his partners in Aaron-Lem. It wasn't Aaron that worried him. Through the years, he had seen how Aaron's greed and need for physical expressions of wealth had weakened the small amount of magic he had once practiced.

Yes, Aaron had once been a master of mental manipulation, but he had turned that practice over to his Preachers, and he no longer was that skilled at it. So perhaps Aaron was controllable, and he could keep Aaron as the fake god, and head of Aaron-Lem. But Sawdi was another story.

Something had changed with Sawdi, or perhaps it had always been there and they had all chosen not to see it. But those Warrior Monks were terrifying. Stryker hoped he never saw them again, or at least not until he had all the pieces of the pendant.

Falcon watched Stryker stumble off and then turned to Captain Kosti.

"Is it time?" Kosti asked.

When Falcon pushed into his mind the answer that it was, the Captain sighed in relief. "Thank the gods. Going this slow with that piece of trash, Stryker, has been the hardest thing the crew and I have ever done.

"We had to slow and stop the ship and still make it look as if we are moving, although it has been fun to keep the boat rocking and watch Stryker get sick.

"Once we drop him off, we are leaving, and getting as far away from Turva as possible. I hope your plan works because otherwise there might not be any place safe for any of us."

As soon as Falcon was off, Captain Kosti made the rounds of the ship speaking quietly to each member of the crew. If Stryker hadn't felt so ill, he might have noticed the wave of relief that passed through the crew of the Soleis. However, he did notice a ceasing of the rocking and the feeling of movement.

At last, he thought. *Falcon was right, as always. We are almost there. Soon, the pendant will be mine.*

****

It didn't take Falcon long to reach the Eos. It still sat calmly in the water while Captain Lira waited to get further instructions from Tarek. If Falcon could have spoken out loud, everyone would have heard him screaming, "What the zonk are you doing?"

Instead, it was Lira who took the brunt of his anger. However, once Lira realized that the Soleis was not that far behind him and was now moving full speed to Turva, he realized his mistake, and within minutes the crew had the ship moving forward again.

By then, Karn had joined the two of them, and he too felt Falcon's anger. "Tarek is not in charge of this plan, Karn," Falcon said.

Karn nodded. "But we need him on board with it," Karn replied.

"Well, get him on board while getting where you are going. Udore, Suzanne, and Rose are on their way and are expecting to meet you there. Tell him that. I have to get back to Edes. The resistance there will be waiting for the sign for us to begin."

None of them had seen Tarek and Meg standing in the doorway until Tarek said, "My father is going to Turva?" followed by Meg asking, "And my sister?"

Falcon turned to Tarek and mind-spoke, "Follow Karn, Tarek, if you want this to work. He knows the plan, and each of you has to do your part." Cocking his head at Meg before flying off, he added, "Especially you, young lady."

"What did he mean by that?" Meg asked, watching Falcon disappear into the sky that was quickly turning gray. She knew no one was going to give her an answer, but at the moment, she didn't care. She and Suzanne would be together again.

All of them felt a moment of relief until Falcon returned, and hovering over them said, "I almost forgot to tell you, Sawdi will be heading there too, just as planned."

Tarek and Meg turned to Karn, and said together, "As planned? What the ziffer? Why?"

NINETEEN

N ow that Tarek was no longer standing in the way of moving the Eos towards Turva, the ship moved through the water as quickly as possible. No longer were they just trying to outrun the Soleis, they were also trying to beat the storm that had appeared on the horizon moments after Falcon had time-shifted away.

"Go below," Captain Lira ordered the four people still standing in his cabin. How he had forgotten that he was in charge of the Eos was beyond him. But now that the storm threatened them, he didn't care if Karn and his friends were upset or not.

This was the first big storm that they had encountered on their trip to Turva. If it was anything like the storms that had been hitting the Islands recently, they were in big trouble. He didn't stop to wonder why one appeared now. He was too busy. Captain Lira knew that the Captain of the Soleis would be moving just as quickly.

For a moment, Lira let himself think about how wonderful it would be if Stryker simply drowned at sea. Maybe one of the crew would push him over into the waves. But Lira knew it wasn't going to happen that way. The crew would be too afraid and too busy trying to survive themselves to attempt to kill one of the most powerful men on Thamon.

Sometimes Lira wondered if they were all crazy. How were they going to defeat Stryker, Aaron, Sawdi, and now the Warrior Monks? He knew that Karn and Falcon had a plan. But how good was it? Did it include all the variables like the storm that was bearing down on them now?

It was still too much to think about at the moment. Instinct took over, and Lira and his crew braced for the storm that was almost on top of them.

****

Below deck, Meg dropped her head in her hands and wondered if she could do anything to help the ship sail smoothly through the storm. If not her, maybe Tarek? Didn't a wizard have powers to help them move faster and escape what was coming?

She was almost afraid to ask him. Ever since Karn had told Tarek that his father was alive and that his cousin Ibris' sister was with him, Tarek acted like someone that she didn't know. Even Silke seemed to be having trouble reaching him. Although Meg had seen Silke try a few times, Tarek had brushed her off.

The whole cabin was avoiding him. Was this a way that wizards should behave? Meg asked herself. Because if it was, then maybe she had a good excuse for being terrified right now.

When Falcon had told them who was meeting them in Turva, Meg had raced through two opposing emotions within seconds. First delight that she would see her sister, Suzanne, again soon, and then abject terror knowing that they could be re-encountering the Warrior Monks.

She barely remembered the first encounter with the Monks. As they all stood together, all the Mages doing all that they could do to cloak the Islands and protect all the inhabitants, she had heard the horrible hum of the Warrior Monks growing louder as they spread out over the Islands.

All she remembered was growing warm, and then someone had pushed her into the circle of Mages. Later she had found out that it was Karn. He had seen the fire surround her and then knew what to do. How had he known? What if the circle of Mages had not been there? Would she have burned up instead of producing a beam of light? And what did the light mean?

While Meg wondered what to do about Tarek, Wren and Karn were sitting across from Meg, whispering together. Meg was happy to see the two of them working out whatever had separated them before. If Wren now trusted her husband, then the rest of them could too. At that moment, Karn said something that had turned Wren's face a bright red. She pushed herself up, gave Karn one of her looks, and then clapped her hands together.

Avoiding looking at Tarek, Wren said, "It looks like I need to take charge again. Leon, could you and your men go up and help the crew with the ship? I am sure they could use some strong arms to batten things down in case we don't outrun the storm."

Wren waited until they had all filed out, and then huffed. "Seriously, why did I have to tell them to do that? We are all grown-ups here. And we are in trouble if everyone doesn't pull their own without needing to be asked to do it."

Wren looked at each person still in the room. When she reached Tarek, she paused and said, "Tarek, stop it. Get over yourself. So your father chose to stay in prison. So what? There was a reason. He didn't abandon you, which is probably what you are telling yourself. He chose this path. This plan. And he is going to need all your powers as a wizard to help him.

"And we need you more than ever, too. We have to get to Turva before the storm, before the Soleis, and before Sawdi and the Warrior Monks. Can you get us there?"

When Tarek dropped his head and stared at the floor, Wren pointed to Meg and gestured for her to do something. Then Wren stood and led everyone else out of the cabin, leaving the two of them alone. When even Silke left the room, Meg was astonished. How could she do anything?

But looking at Tarek, who had been so strong and commanding, staring at the floor, softened her heart and strengthened her resolve.

He had helped her. She could help him. So, she did the only thing she knew to do. She went to him and put her arm around him. At first, he stiffened up, and then he put his head on her shoulder.

She whispered to him, "It's going to be all right, Tarek."

It surprised Meg to realize that she wasn't just saying those words. She believed them with all her heart.

"I should have known," Tarek mumbled.

"There was a reason you didn't, Tarek. I am sure of that. Just as I am sure that there is a reason why I am here on Thamon. But we will only find out that reason if we do everything we know how to do at this moment, and I am sure you know how to get us to Turva faster."

Tarek raised his head and looked into Meg's green eyes. She was no longer the wild-child and self-serving woman he had first met that day on the Islands. He still remembered the meadow, and the joy he felt at being there, despite why he had come.

His father and his cousin Rose were alive. Maybe they all were. But they were a long way to finding out the answer. First, he needed to get them all safely to Turva.

Tarek nodded at Meg and then leaned over and kissed her on the cheek. She had become his rock and guiding star. The least he could do was save her.

Meg smiled at him, and for that moment, he was sure she was right. They were here together for a reason.

TWENTY

The storm that was racing after the ships heading to Turva was also hovering around the Islands. Ibris thought it felt as if the storm was trying to decide whether to punish the Islands or let them be. The sky had turned black, and lightning flashed out to sea. But the rain and wind had not yet hit the Islands.

As the Preacher, Ibris had once been the only one that had to make sure that the Arrow was clear and people safe in their homes before the storms hit. Now that the few Mages that had survived were back out among the people again, they took back their responsibilities. Ibris was sure that was one reason that the storm hovered offshore. The Mages were doing what they once did, calming the storm as much as possible. They would let just enough rainfall on the Islands to keep them lush and productive.

Gratitude for what had happened on the Islands to make it free again filled Ibris' heart. Yes, they had work to do to bring the Islands back to what they once were. They also had to find a new path that included those who wanted to continue to worship Aaron-Lem.

Oiseon, the elected leader of the Mages, Ruth, Roar, and Samis, were meeting with Ibris. Dax no longer came to meetings. He gave many reasons for staying away, but Ibris knew it was because the people didn't believe in him and were still angry at what he had done. Dax didn't think that he had a place where violence was not needed or wanted. The more Dax and Ibris talked about it, the more sure Dax was that he didn't belong on the Islands. He needed to do something.

"I should have left on the ship with Stryker," Dax often said.

Ibris would argue that Stryker would have killed him, and Dax would argue back that he wouldn't have. And even if Stryker did try to kill him, Dax would have made sure that he took Stryker with him.

"At least it would have given me something to do," Dax would say.

It was because of Dax that the five of them were meeting. As they watched the storm move out to sea, only dropping enough rain to feed the Islands, Oiseon turned to Ibris and asked, "Are we going to say yes to Dax? And if we do, does that mean that we trust him?"

"I don't see that we have a choice," Ibris said. "He is going to do it with or without us. As far as trusting him, no, we can't. I say that loving Dax. But something is broken inside of him, and I am not sure that what he says he wants to do is what he will end up doing."

"Could you tell us again what he wants to do?" Ruth asked. "And what exactly does he want from us?"

"He wants to go to the Palace and kill Aaron. He says he can do it. I think he probably can. But why? Because he wants to take Aaron's place?" Ibris asked.

"I know that for years he has planned to be more powerful. I suspect he has wanted to take power away from Aaron, Stryker, and Sawdi. Although I have no idea how he thought he was going to do that without help. But still. I do believe he could kill Aaron.

"I've heard that Aaron has become soft and cares too much about wealth and riches. However, if we endorse this and help Dax, then we also are responsible for killing Aaron, which I no longer want to be part of on any level. Besides, some people will take his death and turn him into something bigger than he already is. His teachings will remain powerful if people see him as a martyr. It doesn't seem wise."

"But as you said," Roar interjected, "How can we stop him? And is it possible to make Thamon free without killing, or at least imprisoning the ones that have enslaved it?"

Oiseon cleared his throat, and everyone turned to listen to what he had to say. After all, he represented the Mages. And Dax had been responsible for imprisoning and killing many of their families and friends.

"I have spoken with the Mages. We know that harboring hate and resentment towards anyone, including Dax, will only weaken us. The enemy that we take revenge on will defeat us, even if we kill them. So we will have no part of revenge.

"But of course we believe in protection. We can protect Dax and help him get to Edes, but we will not support the killing of Aaron. Would Dax agree to only stopping him, and not killing him?"

"I agree," Dax said from the doorway.

"You aren't supposed to be here, Dax," Ibris said.

"And yet, you are discussing me as if I am a specimen. I have a say in this too. Yes, I heard your discussion. You forget that I was, maybe still am, the head of the most influential Kai-Via in Thamon. My six men were not personal friends to me, but Sawdi killed them just because he felt like it.

"Do you want a man like that coming after you? I know Tarek and the others think they can stop him. Perhaps they can. Maybe they can prevent Stryker from recovering the pendant.

"But even if they do all that, what power does Aaron still have? He will never want to be anything less than a god. Someone has to do something about him. Let it be me. I will imprison him if I can. I won't go to kill him.

"Yes, I wanted to be all-powerful. But I have watched what that looks like, and it no longer appeals to me. However, I cannot turn into something I am not. I am a warrior. You haven't asked Ibris to stop being a preacher. Perhaps I am a better man now than I was before, but I still need to fight.

"I chose the winning side. And the fact that I am choosing your side should give you hope. I think you will be on the winning side. Let me fight for it.

"Help me get to Edes and Aaron's Palace. I can't promise you many things, but I can promise you that you'd rather have me there than here."

Ibris stood and walked to Dax and put his arms around him. Dax stood stiffly for a moment and then reluctantly hugged Ibris back. Ibris whispered in his ear, "I love you, brother."

Dax didn't respond. But it was those words that would drive him forward into his destiny. It was the only way he could tell Ibris that he loved him, too. Dax thought Ibris would understand.

TWENTY ONE

The Warrior Monk was back in the corner of Aaron's room and followed him wherever he went. Who knew if it was the same one? They all looked alike. If Sawdi's plan was to drive Aaron crazy, it was working.

Besides the Monk that followed him everywhere, Sawdi had his army of Warrior Monks camped outside the doors of the Palace. Although they were quiet at the moment, their presence was still terrifying, which Aaron figured was the point that Sawdi was making. He was angry, and he wasn't going to let Aaron forget it.

Aaron had thought that Sawdi would leave immediately to chase after Udore, but Sawdi was still there, or at least Aaron assumed that he was since the Monks were, and Sawdi was the only one who controlled them.

But Aaron hadn't seen Sawdi since the day before when he had stormed out of the throne room. Aaron shuddered at the memory. That morning, as Aaron dressed, he saw the bruises that ran down the side of his body where he had bounced and then slid across the floor.

The floor still had gouges and scratches in it. The Blessed Ones couldn't fix it, and the men who had initially laid the floor were nowhere to be found, so he had no idea how long it would be before the floor would look perfect again.

If Falcon were around, he would send him out to find the man. But getting past the Monks might be tricky, even for Falcon.

Aaron hated to admit it, but the truth was, he was a prisoner in his own Palace. Falcon was missing. His women were gone. Things were not as they should be. And he felt powerless to do anything about it.

Aaron sat on his throne, thinking about what he could do. Although he would miss the women, they weren't what he was the most upset about. It was the children. They were his. They, and their future, belonged to him.

His children would be the new Thamon. He was training them to be the new Preachers and Kai-Via to replace Stryker's imperfect ones. Because no matter how good the current Preachers and Kai-via were, the world they grew up in had influenced them.

His children would be pure, not sullied by being human or by other people, especially mothers and fathers. He was God. They were the children of God. All they knew was Aaron-Lem. They would control the world long after he was gone. It was his legacy.

Yes, he could always get more women, but he couldn't replace his children. He had to find them. But locked inside the Palace with the humming, swirling mass of white wraiths surrounding him, he had no way to search for them.

Aaron knew that he had to find the children before Sawdi did. Because if Sawdi found the children first, he would eliminate them, and then it would take him years to get back to where he was now.

Aaron called the Blessed One standing by the door to come closer. The Blessed One shuffled forward until he stood directly in front of Aaron's throne.

As often as Aaron had seen them do that, it still impressed him. Their training had been impeccable. Perhaps it would be wise to reward their teachers, Aaron thought, and then changed his mind. No, that would only encourage them to want more. It was best to let things remain the same, at least the ones that he still controlled.

Although Aaron assumed that the Warrior Monk could hear him anyway, Aaron leaned forward and whispered in the Blessed

One's ear, "Bring me Baywolf once the Warrior Monks and Sawdi leave."

The Blessed One nodded and shuffled out of the room. Aaron leaned back into his chair, carved from a massive tree. Among the glitter of the room, it felt out of place. But Aaron had wanted people to know that he ruled all of Thamon, not just the people, but everything that grew.

It was true he felt defeated at the moment, but he did have some secrets that Sawdi hadn't learned about yet, or if he did, they wouldn't look dangerous to him.

It was good that he had kept Stryker's replacement close by and a secret, Aaron mused. Baywolf had been at Stryker's training camp, and Aaron had met him on one of his visits. Stryker was in the process of discarding the boy. He didn't like the way he looked. Stryker thought the boy had an ugly face. But it wasn't only his looks that had turned Stryker away. It was the boy's inability to follow directions.

But Aaron had seen something that Stryker had not. The boy, who then was called Bay, couldn't hear, and that's why he didn't obey orders. It also made him a good servant for Aaron, so he had asked to be given Bay, and Stryker had agreed. It was an easy way to get rid of him.

Bay had earned the second half of his name after Aaron caught him attacking a member of his staff who had hit him and knocked him to the floor. Bay attacked the man with such ferocity that it reminded Aaron of a wolf. When Aaron stood by and let him beat the man, Bay had turned to Aaron, bowed, and said, "I serve only you, my God."

Aaron had nodded and then brought the newly named Baywolf to the Palace and began to train him. With that kind of loyalty and fighting ability, he would be good to have around.

Over time, Aaron discovered that Baywolf could hear, just chose not to unless it was Aaron. His ability to hear remained their secret, along with how well trained he was, and how big he had gotten.

Only the blind Blessed Ones were ever allowed in Baywolf's presence, so no one knew what Baywolf had become.

Once Sawdi was gone, the two of them would work out a way to take Thamon back from both Stryker and Sawdi. He and Baywolf had been waiting many years for that day, and it was almost here.

Twenty Two

W hat Aaron didn't know was that Sawdi was not in the Palace. First, Sawdi had taken Bolong to the cavern and released the Warrior Monks and left them to guard the Palace. Then Sawdi had headed to his cabin in the mountains.

He needed time to think through what had happened and what he wanted to do next. Yes, he needed to follow Udore, but he knew where Udore was going. He could follow him later.

Yes, he was surprised that Udore had escaped, and he had been furious. But the more he thought about it, the more Sawdi decided that perhaps this was a better way for all this to happen. He could stay out of the fray until they were all on Turva. Maybe the rebels could stop Stryker and his plans with the pendant. If the rebels failed, he could come in and save the day and get rid of all the Mages and Stryker at the same time.

In the meantime, he had Aaron trapped in the Palace. He could decide what to do with him later. Sawdi's plan all along was to let Aaron continue to be the figurehead for Aaron-Lem, but the ring kept urging him to kill him instead.

It was another reason Sawdi had left the Palace. The anger he had felt towards Aaron had surprised him. The ring had taken over. He felt the white rage rise, and before he knew it, the person he believed himself to be vanished and a deep dark presence rose within him.

Yes, Sawdi knew he was not a good man. He did love to harm people and do bad things. He did enjoy torturing and controlling people. But the dark presence that took over his actions and his thinking was much more than just bad. It was pure evil, and Sawdi had to use all his strength to keep it from destroying not only Aaron but the Palace and everyone in it.

The dark presence and the anger that came with it had no reason or logic. It just wanted to destroy. Sawdi knew it was the ring.

Not for the first time since he had placed it on his finger, Sawdi wished that he had never found it. Before the ring, what he had valued the most was his ability to be the master of his thinking and his emotions. Not only his, but all of those around him. But the ring was taking over all of it.

What he wanted to do was take the ring off. But every time that thought occurred to him, a blinding flash of pain swept through his entire body, making him incapable of moving. So Sawdi had returned to the cabin to seek some silence, and to keep that evil from having a reason to lash out. Sawdi was aware that his ability to make that kind of choice might also be fading. Would who he was be swallowed up by the dark being that lived within him now?

Sawdi knew that Stryker was after a pendant that Stryker believed would make him ruler of all of Thamon. But what if the pendent ruled Stryker just as the ring was ruling him now?

Had the pendant and the ring been made by the same person? Yes, he knew the myth about the pendant. The sky god, Tewao, made it and gave it to his son. The son had used it for evil, so Tewao broke it apart and hid the pieces. Maybe the pendant took over the son like the ring was taking over him?

But the god part didn't fit for Sawdi. He knew men created their gods. So perhaps a powerful being that others called god made the pendant. But why not destroy it? Why only hide it? And why a map?

Did the same "god" make the ring? Why was it him who found it? Was all this preordained?

That's when Sawdi thought about the prophecies. He had never read them, but he had heard they existed. Since he felt as if he made his own fate, he had never cared about them before. He had thought of the prophecies as fantasy. Something others made up to help them understand the unexplainable.

But what if those prophecies gave him a way to take off the ring? Maybe not destroy it, but at least make it stop leading him around, taking away his free will.

Perhaps he should go to Turva sooner than he had planned. He had heard that was where the people had hidden the written pages. How printed pages could survive over thousands and thousands of years was a mystery, but not one bigger than a ring that demanded things of him.

The ring had let him come to the cabin. Maybe giving him a rest or perhaps it needed time to rest too. Although Sawdi was tempted to think about taking the ring off, he didn't want to risk that it was still there waiting to punish him. If he went to Turva, the ring would think it was for revenge. Perhaps he could hide that he was also looking for answers.

Sawdi stood and walked to the door of his cabin. Bolong was waiting patiently for him at the edge of the woods. How did Udore get away? Sawdi wondered. He didn't ride any of the dragons. Maybe Bolong had turned him down. That's what Sawdi wanted to believe. He needed something to be loyal to him. Why not Bolong?

Turning back to look at his quiet cabin, Sawdi sighed. As much as he would like more quiet time, other things took priority. As he climbed onto Bolong for the ride back to the Palace, Sawdi wondered again how did Udore leave? It disturbed him that he had missed so many things. It was time to pay more attention.

Digging his heels into Bolong's neck, he decided to fly the normal way back to the Palace. It gave him more time with his thoughts. Maybe he would find an elegant way to get rid of all the people, the pendant and the ring, all at the same time.

Twenty Three

T he storm passed over Eos without touching it. Not because the storm wasn't raging around them, but because they passed through it as if they were in a transparent tunnel.

Tarek had come up to the deck, raised his hands to the black sky, mumbled something, and everything went quiet. Standing inside the transparent tunnel, they could see the lightning flash and the pounding rain. They could even see the waves rise up and over them, but nothing touched them or the Eos.

Within minutes, they were outside the tunnel, and the sky was blue without any sign of wind or rain. Although waves still rocked the ship, they were nothing like the waves that had threatened them before.

In the distance, Meg could see land. The crew cheered and then went back to what they were doing as if nothing had happened.

"They don't remember," Tarek answered Meg's unspoken question. "It's best that they don't repeat that story."

Meg didn't have time to question why, because Tarek, with Silke on his shoulder, hurried off to talk to Captain Lira about where he wanted to have the ship dock. Leon and his men were busy helping the crew, and Meg wondered if they didn't remember either. Wren and Karn were still below. Meg assumed they were talking about their relationship, or maybe Karn was telling Wren more of the larger plan.

That left Meg alone on the deck, looking out over the waves and wondering about the next part of their journey when she heard the roar of a dragon. Her heart leaped. Was it Suzanne? A few seconds later, her sister, as Lady the dragon, flew into view, spit out a blast of fire into the waves, tipped her wings, and headed to shore.

Tarek must have heard the roar because he burst out of the Captain's cabin and swept Meg up in his arms. The two of them embraced with tears flowing down their cheeks. Suzanne had returned, and on her back were two people. "My father and Rose," Tarek had breathed.

Silke arrived moments later and perched on Tarek's shoulder, watching where Lady flew towards Turva. Tears were running down Silke's cheeks, too.

For the moment, there was nothing wrong in the world. People that they loved were safe, the sky was blue, and as Etar and Trin crossed each other, the blue flash confirmed that it was a good day.

Passing through time the way that they had done, they were far ahead of the Soleis. Besides, the storm would also slow Stryker down. It gave them a little time to begin the search for the pendant piece before he arrived.

Although Meg had asked Tarek more than once if he knew where that piece was, he had never answered the question. She would have to trust him. Otherwise, what good would it do to be the first on land?

As the shore drew closer, the crew lowered the rowboats. They would row everyone to land and then move the Eos to the town of Yeal Thalor, where it would dock. The village would be expecting them as a trading ship.

The small harbor where Lira had brought the rebels was unknown to most people. And it was where Lira had also brought the Mages and their families on his last trip.

From there, the Mages would have walked to the coordinates where the other refugees were hiding. Vald knew the coordinates of the Sanctuary because Leon and Tarek had given them to him before he left the Islands.

But getting to the Sanctuary would not have been easy. The Mages and their families would have had to avoid people. They couldn't follow the roads or trails or stop in towns for supplies. Their path would have taken them up into the mountains.

Members of Lira's crew were also going ashore with the rebels, but not to help find the pendant. They would be heading to the Sanctuary to bring supplies. Tarek and Leon would give them coordinates after they reached the shore. No one wanted to take any chances that the remaining crew going to the village of Yeal Thalor would give the Sanctuary away even by mistake. Even Lira didn't know, and he wanted it to be that way.

The hours that it took to get to shore felt to Meg longer than the entire trip had taken. And she knew that Tarek felt the same way. Although they had seen Lady and her two passengers land onshore, after her sister shifted back to being Suzanne, the three of them had waved and then headed inland.

Meg knew that they were waiting out of sight, but the fact that she could no longer see them made it even harder. However, she and Tarek had decided to be the last ones off the ship. So as they watched their friends make their way to shore and then disappear into the trees, they stood quietly together, holding hands.

For both of them, just holding hands was a brand new experience. Tarek had never had any interest in a woman, and Meg had been too busy thinking only of herself to care about someone else, let alone a man. The fact that Tarek was a wizard and she was becoming something other than a shapeshifter had first stopped Meg from allowing herself to feel more for Tarek.

But after almost losing Tarek and all her friends to the Warrior Monks and Sawdi, something snapped open in her heart. Perhaps the fire and the light beam had been part of what happened, but all Meg knew was she was ready to admit that what she felt was love.

So holding hands was more than just that they were united in their fight against the three men who wanted to rule Thamon.

Neither of them could see Silke sitting on Tarek's shoulder watching the shoreline. She smiled to herself. It all went well; she was thinking, she would someday have another wizard to shepherd through life.

But first, they had to succeed in destroying the pendant and the ring. Silke sighed to herself. Yes, she knew about the ring. Karn had told her, but he had only confirmed what she had already known. After all, this had all been written in the prophecies. What wasn't written was how it ended.

That was up to them.

Twenty Four

O n the Soleis, Stryker wept. No one saw him because he was below deck in his cabin. And he wasn't weeping because he was sad. He cried from fear. Would they survive the storm? It was horrendous.

Captain Kosti had seemed unconcerned. But then he and his crew had lashed themselves to the ship to keep from being swept overboard. Kosti had given Stryker a choice. Stay on deck and be bound to the ship, or go below and wait it out.

So, despite being sicker than he had ever remembered being, or thought possible, Stryker went below. He knew he would have wept on deck too, and there was no way he was going to show that weakness to anyone, let alone the crew of the Soleis.

He had crawled beneath his bunk, dragging blankets and pillows with him, trying to block out hearing the wind and rain pounding the Soleis while throwing it back and forth like a toy. For the thousandth time, he promised himself that he would never, ever take a boat again.

Of course, once he found the pendant, he wouldn't have to. He would have the power of the gods. He could stay in one place and command a world.

The day he found the map he could never have imagined where it would take him. At seven, he had no idea what his life would be like. But despite how it felt at the moment, and the fear and illness that was sweeping through every cell of his body, Stryker knew that he wouldn't change a thing. Someday it would all be worth it.

One thing that the storm was doing for him was keeping his mind off of who would be coming after him. He knew that sooner or later Sawdi, and probably the Warrior Monks, would track him down. But once he had the pendant, all would be well. The last time he felt well enough to look at the map, it still showed him that the middle of the pendant was on Turva. Not exactly where it was, just the general area. It had been the same on the Islands.

The map had sent him there, and once he arrived, it started showing him where on the Islands to find the pieces. Stryker knew that once he got to Turva, it would show him where to go next. Captain Kosti said they would be docking in the harbor at Yeal Thalor. From there, he was on his own.

Stryker moaned and held his ears, trying to keep out the shrieking wind. It reminded him of the shrieking of the Warrior Monks. Knowing Sawdi, he probably made them sound that way on purpose. Storm or Monks, it was terrifying.

Suddenly the shrieking and pounding stopped, and the ship calmed to a slow roll. Stryker sighed and rolled out from beneath his bunk, needing to do so before a crew member came down and found him wrapped in blankets on the floor.

He had made it to the edge of the bunk and smoothed out his hair before a crew member stuck his head into the cabin and announced that they were through the storm, and they could see land ahead.

Stryker flicked his wrist at him to go and pulled himself off the bed. Making his way across the cabin, he looked at his reflection in the mirror and shook his head. He was a mess. He brushed his hair, straightened his clothes, checked for the pendant piece hanging around his neck, and felt for the one sewed into his cloak.

As long as he had those two things, he would be okay. Better than okay. He was one step closer to being the ruler of Thamon.

Up on deck, the air smelled wonderful. The storm had washed away all the nasty smells of the ship and the men. The only bad smell was coming from him, but there was nothing he could do about that for now. Ahead, Stryker could see the town of Yeal Thalor coming into view.

Everyone left Stryker alone as they busied themselves, preparing to dock in the village's harbor. Stryker noticed that if they had the choice, they were all upwind of him. He thought about moving so that they were all downwind, but he still felt too weak to bother. They were nothing to him, why would he waste energy on annoying them this way.

Once he was the one ruler, he could always reach out and punish them. No one would be off-limits then. But for now, all he wanted was to be rid of them all and on his way before Sawdi arrived.

Now that the ship was almost at its destination, Stryker felt well enough to think back to what had happened on the Islands.

He had betrayed all of them, including Dax, Ibris, and that wizard Tarek and his rebels. Stryker chuckled to himself, his energy starting to return. He had left all of them on the Islands to be destroyed by Sawdi and his Monks. Or maybe by the storm that had arrived at the same time.

No matter what, they were all dead. That made his life so much easier. All he had to do was outwit Aaron and Sawdi. Stryker wasn't worried about Aaron. Aaron would be too busy maintaining his superiority and wealth. Besides, Aaron hated ships even more than he did, and Sawdi would never let him ride one of his dragons. No, all he had to worry about was Sawdi.

Watching the village come into view, Stryker felt more and more like himself. He would take over one of those houses he could see lining the streets of Yeal Thalor.

What a name for a village, Stryker thought. It was probably named after some god or two. He'd have to rename it because it was where he had come to claim his heritage. The village, maybe the city, of Stryker. It sounded good to him.

Behind him, Captain Kosti gestured to two members of the crew to lower the rowboat. It was time to get Stryker off his ship and for them to sail away from Turva as quickly as possible. In fact, they were heading back to the Islands. Right now, that might be the safest place on the planet.

Although Stryker believed that the Islands and the people had been destroyed, Falcon had assured Kosti that their plan had worked. So, once they gathered food and supplies, they would be sailing as fast as they had ever sailed, away from Turva. Away from the coming battle between men who wanted to be gods.

TWENTY FIVE

Meg and Tarek turned and waved at the retreating Eos. They could see a few members of the remaining crew waving back. "Will they be okay?" Meg asked. "They'll be in Yeal Thalor when Stryker gets there."

Silke was the one who answered her. She had flown out of the woods to greet them, and heard the question. "Stryker doesn't know that you survived, or that the Eos had anything to do with any of the rescues.

"Captain Lira is smart. He won't stay in that harbor for long. Lira is taking a few men and moving the ship. There is another small hidden harbor on the other side of Yeal Thalor, where he said he'd wait in case he was needed."

"Doesn't he want to return to a family?" Meg asked, once again, surprising herself that caring about family was something that meant something to her.

"He says that his crew, and now the rebels and refugees are his family," Silke replied.

Tears rushed to Meg's eyes. Someday she would find a way to thank him, she thought. Tarek squeezed her hand, and she knew he understood what she was thinking.

"Are you ready?" Silke asked the two of them. With one last look at the retreating Eos, they turned to follow Silke into the woods, where the rest of the rebels and the crew that had come with them had gathered.

Although neither of them spoke about it out loud, both Tarek and Meg were wondering if Suzanne, Udore, and Rose were waiting for them, too. Silke turned to look at the two of them as if they were crazy.

"Of course they are, you two zonking idiots."

Meg glanced at Tarek, putting her hand on his arm, and he smiled. He knew what she was asking: could he take them there now?

Within seconds they were standing a few yards away from a group of people gathered around a fire. Although the warm season had arrived, there was still a leftover chill in the air. And even if there hadn't been, they probably would have built a fire anyway.

There is nothing quite as welcoming as a roaring fire, Meg thought as she scanned the crowd. Then Suzanne turned to her, and both of them took off running towards each other.

As they hugged, Suzanne realized that her sister had grown into a beautiful young woman, and she felt a pang of sorrow knowing that their parents would never have a chance to see what their youngest daughter had become.

Although Tarek wanted to rush at his father, the same way that Suzanne and Meg had done, he was afraid to move. Part of him still felt angry that his father had not told him that he was alive. That Udore had left him thinking that he had to stop Aaron-Lem's takeover of Thamon all by himself, or at least with the rebels that he could gather.

And then there was Silke. She must have known that Udore was alive. But she willingly transferred her allegiance to him, leaving his father alone with Aaron. All those thoughts kept Tarek from moving forward, but it didn't stop Udore, who ran to Tarek and threw his arms around him.

"My son," he said, stepping back to look into his eyes, his hands staying on Tarek's shoulders.

Tarek looked into his father's blue eyes, so like his own, and saw the pain and sorrow that lived there, and finally broke down and hugged his father. Then the two of them walked to Rose, who was waiting for them by the fire. Tarek pulled her into his embrace with Udore.

"Your brother doesn't know that you are alive, Rose. I know he mourns you. Despite being trained as a Preacher, or maybe because of it, you know he helped save the Islands."

Rose nodded. "I'm sorry that there was no way to tell him. Aaron had us all locked away, and we had to keep him happy to stay alive.

"If Udore hadn't allowed himself to be captured, I would have been blinded, and probably I would have eventually died like so many of my Blessed Ones sisters did. But Udore kept both those things from happening to me.

"If your father hadn't stayed in the palace all this time, none of us would have a chance against those three men."

At Rose's words, the last of Tarek's residual feelings of abandonment fell away. His father had done all of this for all of them.

Tarek realized that, like Meg, he needed to give up his childhood to prepare him to help the resistance. In his father's absence, he had grown into who he had to be.

"Enough of that," Leon shouted across the fire. "Come join us. We have food. We are on land. We are together. Come!"

Udore turned to Tarek. "It's a good idea, son. Stryker won't come looking for you. He thinks you are all dead.

"He will rest for a bit before looking for the pendant, and he doesn't yet know exactly where it is."

"What about Sawdi?" Meg asked as she and Suzanne joined the small group.

As Tarek started to introduce Meg, Udore stopped him. "I know this young woman, or at least I have heard about you, Meg. Your sister couldn't stop talking about you."

Meg smiled at Suzanne and accepted Udore's warm hug, thinking that he had left something out, but she had no idea what it was. "I have heard of you, too, Udore."

Udore turned to everyone and answered Meg's question.

"Sawdi will come for Stryker and me because he knows Turva is where we were all heading. But we have time to rest. And some things need to be said before he arrives. Things you all need to know. It's time."

Udore looked at Silke, who nodded in agreement. "Yes," she said. "It's time."

TWENTY SIX

A lthough Meg loved every minute of that night around the fire, she was restless. There was something that she didn't know yet, and it troubled her. She kept catching Udore and Silke glancing her way, and even Suzanne had a strange look in her eyes. It felt as if there was a secret that they were all keeping that centered around her.

Although she used to believe that the whole world revolved around her, that was in the past. She wasn't that person anymore. So much had changed.

The latest change had happened only a few days before while they were on the Eos. Wren had asked her to fly with her. Meg couldn't. She couldn't shapeshift. At all. To anything.

What surprised Meg is that she hadn't broken down over it. Everyone knew. It was not a secret. Maybe she wasn't upset because her abilities had been fading for a while, and she half expected it to happen. For whatever reason, she was at peace with it. She had watched Wren fly and smiled. Smiled because she wasn't jealous or afraid.

Well, she wasn't afraid of not being a shapeshifter anymore, or at least for now, but she was fearful of what she was becoming. Because what she hadn't told anyone, even Wren, was that sometimes she felt the same way she had felt before being surrounded by the fire. It was a click inside of her, a warm feeling. But then it would pass.

Meg hoped that if she were ever surrounded by fire again, Karn would be nearby to help, since he had seemed to know what to do before. She glanced over at Karn and Wren, sitting together on the other side of the fire, whispering and smiling at each other. Maybe she should ask Karn what was happening to her, or even ask Tarek to help her.

When Udore looked over at Meg and tilted his head, she realized that he knew the answer. That the secret everyone seemed to be keeping did involve her. Meg knew that once again, her life was about to be turned upside down.

Leaning her head against Tarek's shoulder, she smiled at Udore and thought that the morning was soon enough to hear the message that would change everything, again.

****

Captain Kosti couldn't get Stryker off his ship fast enough. He would have rowed him to shore himself if he had thought it would get Stryker there sooner. But his men felt the same, so they almost fought over who would take him.

They decided on the two fastest rowers on the Soleis. Stryker had no idea what was happening. He was hustled into the boat and onto the shore before he could do anything other than collect the few belongings he had escaped with.

The fact that he was one of the most powerful people on Thamon didn't seem to matter to anyone, including Stryker. They all wanted the same thing. Get Stryker off the boat. So Stryker tolerated their hustling him off the Soleis and told himself they were doing it that way because he ordered them to.

Kosti couldn't care less about what Stryker told himself about what was happening. He saluted him and gave him some food from the ship, thinking he probably wouldn't eat it anyway because he might once again worry that his food was poisoned. He helped him into the rowboat, and then turned to his crew who smiled in delight at Stryker's going.

As they waited for the crew members who had gone ashore to get supplies, they started washing every inch of the ship. They didn't want one trace of Stryker on board.

Some of the crew would not be returning, and Kosti understood that they would be searching for the missing families. Falcon had told them about the Eos, and they would join up with the crew from that ship to take supplies to the Sanctuary.

Stryker knew none of this. He never looked back at the Soleis. He hated that ship. He wanted a real bed that didn't move and food that hadn't been prepared by a crew that hated him. Since no one knew him on Yeal Thalor, he was going to remain anonymous. It would be safer. He could walk around the town and eat whatever he wanted without worrying that someone would try and poison him.

Besides, he needed time to study the map and see where it wanted him to go. If he needed to, he would hire a local guide to get him there.

Stopping at one of the stalls on the street that sold food, he asked where to find the best rooming house. The owner pointed to a building located directly across the street.

After checking it out, he decided that it would be comfortable enough while giving him a good view of the main street.

The woman running it had directed him to a room at the end of a long hall, and left him alone, but not before pointing out where he could take a bath. Stryker smirked to himself. Yes, he smelled terrible. But if she knew who he was, she wouldn't have been so blunt about what she wanted him to do.

It didn't matter. She would know when he was ready to tell her. In the meantime, it served Stryker's purpose that she, and everyone else, remained in the dark.

****

Across from the boarding house, two of Leon's men stood watching, Joseph Lead and Fionn Bold. They had volunteered to watch Stryker. Of course, they knew who he was, but he wouldn't remember them. Besides, although they were not going to let him out of their sight, he would never see them.

Their job was to track where he went. If he found out where the pendant was before the rebels, they were to stop him anyway that they could.

If Sawdi came for Stryker, their orders were to get away as fast as possible and let Sawdi and his Warrior Monks do what they wanted with Stryker.

Wren would be keeping in contact with Joseph and Fionn. She would be moving between the three groups of people now on Turva, making sure everyone knew what was happening. Leon and three more of his men were going with the members of Eos and Soleis to the Sanctuary. Yes, they were bringing supplies, but they were also protecting the refugees in case Sawdi, or even Stryker, figured out where they were.

Udore had suggested the extra protection. He knew that Sawdi knew that there were survivors on Turva, which meant that Sawdi, actually the ring, would want them eliminated. Besides, all of them were hoping to find family they hadn't seen for years. If they had survived, that's where they would be.

After seeing Stryker tucked away at the boarding house, Joseph and Fionn settled into a room across the street, taking turns watching, while the other slept. Whatever Stryker would do next, he would never be alone. They would be watching.

Twenty Seven

"How are you planning to get to Edes, Dax?" Ibris asked. The rest of the Council remained silent, waiting for his response.

"I was hoping one of you would have an answer for me," Dax said. "Some kind of magic?"

If Dax had wanted to alienate everyone in the room, he chose the right words. How could he possibly suggest that they use magic to help him? After all, Dax was the man who had captured, tortured, and killed their friends because they were Mages or shapeshifters. Dax was the reason that the valley on Hetale was now underwater. Dax was the reason the twelve Mages rescued from the prison camp had nightmares.

Of all the rescued Mages, only Oiseon wanted to serve on the Council along with Ruth, Roar, Samis, and Ibris. Yes, if Dax wished to leave the Islands, they were delighted, but they weren't going to go out of their way to help him, especially with magic. They stared at him, and he stared back.

Finally, Ibris said, "Dax, how can you ask that? Besides, magic can't just lift you up and take you to Edes. You'll have to wait for a ship to come to the harbor. Even then, it might be hard to get them to take you to Aaron's Palace, although we could certainly try. But, only two captains know that the Islands are still inhabited, Captain Lira and Captain Kosti, and both of them are on the way to Turva. I don't know if either will come back here. And if they do, it won't be for a while."

Dax backed up against the wall and looked at the Council before saying, "I know you hate me. With good reason. But I need to fight. Either I will stay here and get myself in trouble, or I leave and go after at least one of the people that started all of this. I have a weapon that I can use. I can do it. I just need to get there."

"Is it what you used to set off the explosion?" Ruth asked.

Dax nodded. "It is. And Aaron doesn't know that I have it. If I can get to him, I can use it against him."

"What about Sawdi and the Warrior Monks?" Samis asked. "How will you get around them?"

"I doubt that they will be there. Sawdi will leave Aaron alone while he goes after Stryker. I can stop Aaron while he is gone."

"Even if we could get you there, Dax," Ibris said, "I doubt that it will be that easy."

"I don't expect it to be easy, Ibris. I hope it isn't. I want to fight. I might even be able to gather supporters to help me. Falcon and Karn said there are people on Edes who are ready to rebel against Aaron-Lem once the time is right."

Ibris studied Dax. He knew his cousin. He had known all along that Dax needed to be fighting, that Dax was pulled towards the desire for power. If they let him stay on the Islands, Dax might turn against them all again, just to satisfy his need to destroy.

Although the Islanders were doing their best to live with him, they would never fully forgive him. Besides the dissenters on the Islands, the ones who wanted Aaron-Lem to be in power again, might side with Dax, and then they would be at war all over again.

Ibris turned to the four other people sitting around the table, hoping they had an answer. Finally, Roar sighed and said, "I know how to get him to the Palace."

"No, Roar," Ruth said. "You can't. You've done enough."

"Yes. Maybe. I did what needed to be done. And Dax did what he did. And that's the problem. Dax is trying to help us instead of using his desire to hurt against us."

"But he tortured you. He tried to kill you," Ruth said. "How can you help him?"

Roar turned to Ruth and took her hands in his. "Ruth, you and I have been best friends a long time. We have lived through many things together. You know me. You know that I have to help him. Maybe that is what I have been put here on Thamon to do. I don't know. But I do know that I know how to get him to Edes.

"I won't be helping him. I am helping Thamon and the Islands, and you, Ruth, and your family, who remain in hiding because they are still afraid of Dax."

Ruth dropped her head, unable to look at Roar. It was true. Her family would not come out of hiding. The Islands still wore the cloak of fear, and most of it was because of Dax.

Dax had moved away from the wall and knelt beside Roar's chair. "Please. Help me, Roar. I can tell you that I am sorry for what I did to you and all of your friends and family, but I want to make up for it in the only way I know how. Be myself and keep destroying. But not destroy what is good but what is evil. And if that destroys me because I am evil too, it's alright with me. In fact, I will welcome it."

Roar gestured to the empty seat beside him, and Dax sat down and waited. Not patiently. His foot was bouncing, and his fingers tapped the table.

"How are you going to do it, Roar?" Ibris asked.

Roar stood up and backed away until he stood in the middle of the room. "Well," he said, "I am a shapeshifter after all."

A second later, where Roar had been standing, a magnificent dragon appeared and then disappeared, and then Roar was back, laughing at their stunned looks.

"What?" Ruth said, standing up at the table, her chair clanging to the floor. "Why didn't I ever know about that? I never, ever, saw you become a dragon."

Roar walked over to Ruth and hugged her. "I was saving it for when it was needed."

"That's amazing, Roar," Ibris said. "But with Dax on your back, it will be exhausting."

"Not if we travel out of time," Ruth said.

Seeing the look on Roar's face, she added, "Yes, I can do that. Which means I will be going with you."

Ruth turned to Ibris, Oiseon, and Samis and said, "Promise me that you will watch over my family, in case I don't come back."

It was Oiseon who answered, "We promise."

No one tried to convince Ruth that she would come back. They knew that Ruth and Roar would be going to stop Aaron, and wouldn't come back until they did, or die trying.

Twenty Eight

Returning to Edes, Falcon heard the low hum that sounded like thousands of angry bees and wanted more than anything to turn around and never return to the Palace. But he knew that he couldn't do that. He had to continue to be the loyal Falcon that both Aaron and Sawdi expected him to be.

There could be no hint of the part he played in the coming rebellion. The fact that he could hear the terrifying sound of the Warrior Monks meant that the plans were working. The women and children would be in hiding, and if all had gone well, Suzanne, Udore, and Rose were already on Turva.

He would have to remain at the Palace for a while. He was exhausted. Aaron had no idea how many messages he was actually delivering when he sent him out to deliver just one, or spy on someone. However, what he would report back to Aaron would be partially true. He was just leaving out all the other things he had seen and done.

Yes, Stryker was heading towards Turva, not coming to the Palace, but they probably already knew that. Yes, there was no one left on the Islands. That's what he would report, but the full message was, "There is no one left on the Islands that most people can see."

The Mages were doing an excellent job of cloaking the Islands so that it did look deserted now.

Falcon knew the rebellion would succeed, though probably at a high cost. But it would succeed if everyone did their part. And if he didn't die in the process, he thought he would return to the Islands. Even if he could never return to his original form, it would be a beautiful place to live out the rest of his life as a Falcon. But first, they had to stop the three men who believed themselves to be invincible.

So as much as he didn't want to hear, or see, the Warrior Monks, their presence was expected. Falcon knew that Sawdi would also want a report from him, and it would be harder to hide the truth from Sawdi than it was from Aaron. He would have to be very careful. But once he reported to the two of them, and rested, he would be free to head out into Edes and monitor how the rest of the plan was progressing.

Falcon knew very little about the prophecies. All he knew was that they existed, that the signs they had spoken about had arrived, and that the woman who would provide the final solution was in place. Falcon had a suspicion who that woman was, but if it were true, she had no idea who she was and that she was necessary for their success. Hopefully, she remained safe until the time was right, because Falcon suspected that they wouldn't succeed unless she did her part.

****

Partially hidden behind one of the spires jutting up off the roof, the man called Baywolf stood watching as he had every day for years. Today he watched the bird everyone called Falcon circle the Palace, obviously looking for some place to land away from the Warrior Monks.

Baywolf didn't blame him. Those freaking dead people turned into white wraiths with empty dark holes for eyes terrified him too. And the fact that the crazy man, Sawdi, was the only one that controlled them made them even more horrifying.

Finding a way to destroy the Warrior Monks was something that Aaron had given Baywolf to study. So far, he had found nothing. Well, Baywolf had discovered something. But he wasn't planning to share that with Aaron.

Baywolf knew that Sawdi's power was changing. It was becoming more potent and more dangerous, if that was possible. Baywolf thought the change was not something Sawdi was doing. It was the ring. Watching from hidden places in the Palace, Baywolf had seen the ring glow. Once the ring shot out a beam of light and narrowly missed where he had been hiding.

That had scared the ziffer out of him. Sawdi hadn't noticed him, but the ring had. So what Baywolf knew was that not only was it Sawdi that they had to get rid of, it was also the ring. Or maybe just the ring.

Was it the ring that had turned so many of his friends into something else? Or did Sawdi have some magic of his own? Yes, Baywolf knew that Falcon used to be one of his classmates at Stryker's training camp, along with the five dragons. Luckily, Aaron had saved him from Sawdi's rage; otherwise, he would probably be like them, unable to return to their original form.

However, no one would recognize Baywolf now. He had grown. Now, he was a man. He was no longer the boy who pretended not to hear. He was taller and stronger than any of the three men ruling Thamon. Including Aaron.

Baywolf laughed to himself. It wasn't hard to be bigger than Aaron. Aaron had become smaller over the years. He had turned his focus to physical wealth instead of improving himself. He had too many servants, too many women, too many interests that did not build him up but drained him.

Baywolf had tried to tell Aaron what he saw happening, but Aaron didn't care. Aaron had that weapon he hid on his wrist and the belief that he had accepted as real. The belief that he was God.

"Who would dare to disobey me?" Aaron would say. "I am their God."

Baywolf knew that many people knew that it was a lie, and sooner or later, they would come after him. But Aaron said that Baywolf was his secret weapon, so he wasn't worried.

Aaron was correct. Baywolf was a secret. And he was a weapon. But Baywolf was more of a weapon than even Aaron knew, and he planned on keeping it that way until it was necessary to use what he had made himself into.

Falcon finally landed, and Baywolf ducked out of sight. He had been watching Falcon for a while now. Instinct told him that Falcon was up to something, and it was not what Aaron had asked of him.

Soon he would find out from his old friend which side he was on. For his sake, Baywolf hoped Falcon was on the same side as him.

Twenty Nine

S uzanne couldn't sleep. Her mind kept rolling around and around the story that she had to tell in the morning. So instead of sleeping, Suzanne lay on the ground, wrapped in blankets looking up at the stars.

Although the arrangement of the stars was entirely different from where she had come from, the view created the same feeling. Amazement at the grandeur and scale of it all, an incomprehensible immensity. Could it be possible to ever understand how all of it had been created?

The question that was keeping her awake was the idea that although the universes were vast beyond comprehension—and she and her sister were on a new planet in the middle of a universe that might not even be the one they had come from—Thamon just might share a common story with the one that had influenced the two dimensions she knew on Gaia–Erda and Earth.

The only way to find out was to talk about it with the others and find out what they knew. Whatever they discovered, she knew one thing for sure. It wasn't by mistake that Meg had been sent to Thamon. And it wasn't a mistake that Suzanne had followed her.

A few hours later, Suzanne woke as Etar broke over the horizon. Etar's rising and setting was almost everyone's favorite times of the day. Without the bright light of Trin, the world was a lovely shade of purple or blue, making everything appear magical.

Leon was bustling around the fire, making something for everyone to eat. No matter where they were, Leon always managed to come up with delicious meals. Suzanne knew that they would all miss him when he left with the others to take supplies and protection to the Sanctuary.

Silke landed beside Suzanne's head and whispered, "It's good that you got a few hours of sleep, Suzanne."

"Were you awake, too?" Suzanne asked.

Silke nodded. "Wren was, too."

"Do you know what I want to talk about?" Suzanne asked.

"We think we do. And then both of us have something to add. And we need to do it before the men leave for the Sanctuary."

Suzanne nodded, rolled over, and groaned as she sat up. She was used to sleeping on the ground, but if she had a choice, she preferred a big fluffy bed in a warm room.

Not likely that will happen anytime soon, she thought to herself.

With all the people helping, it didn't take long until everyone was fed, the fire put out, and the campsite restored to what it had looked like before they had descended upon it.

The men from the Eos and Soleis had distributed packs of food to everyone, but most of it was going to the Sanctuary so they and Leon and his men would be carrying large bundles on their back.

The group retreated to a small clearing deeper in the woods. They wanted to be a little less visible in case someone was looking for them. Although Wren had come back from town and said that Stryker looked as if he would be staying in town for the day, and Joseph and Todd would keep him in their sights, it was still wise to be cautious.

Once everyone had settled in, sitting on their packs, or rocks, Tarek turned to Suzanne and said, "Silke said we need to begin with what you want to tell us."

Suzanne took a deep breath and began. "Part of me feels crazy telling you this story. But the more I think about the pendant, the more I wonder if it is the work of two brothers.

"On Erda, one of our own, Aki, used to tell this strange story. And as we worked to overthrow Abbadon, the evil man trying to take over Erda, we discovered that the story—at least for Erda—was true."

Turning to Meg, Suzanne said, "You weren't there when we overcame what they had done. It happened when mom and dad took you away from Erda. Besides, after it was over, only a few of us retained the memory.

"The story, as Aki told it, was that there were two brothers. Aki called them the two bored brothers who had traveled the universe, or maybe more than one universe, on a snake-shaped silver spaceship.

"Their home planet had been destroyed, and to keep themselves from going crazy, they decided to experiment with the evolution of planets that they discovered on their travels.

"As I understand it, they tried different experiments on these planets. On Gaia, they experimented with the two dimensions of Earth and Erda."

It was Rose who asked the question. "So you think that these two bored brothers experimented with Thamon? With the pendant?"

"It makes sense, doesn't it? We don't really believe the story that a god named Tewao made a pendant, gave it to his son who then abused its power. Then Tewao took it back, broke it in thirds, buried it, and then made some kind of 'magical' map that would allow someone to find it?

"But the brothers would have done that as an experiment. They would have wanted to see what people would do with it.

"On Gaia, they were testing the powers of good and evil. They wanted to know which side would win. Would greed override love?

"Why wouldn't they use something like a pendant that makes the wearer all-powerful to do the same on Thamon?

"As we know, Stryker has chosen greed. The contest between those of us representing good, and the three men that represent the desire to rule everyone and everything on Thamon, would be exactly what the brothers would have set up. If they ever made it back to Thamon, they would study the outcome of their experiment."

"So you are saying that these brothers got their kicks studying these things because they saw us as nothing compared to them?" Rose asked. "That all that has happened, the destruction, the killing, our imprisonment, all the evil that has swept through Thamon, could be a result of two freaking brothers who didn't know what to do with themselves other than cause upheaval and death? Are you zonking kidding me?"

Rose turned to Udore, who had sat quietly while Suzanne told the story. "Tell me that this isn't true," she demanded.

Instead of answering, Udore looked over at Silke and Wren.

"It fits," Wren said.

"Fits with what?" Rose demanded.

"The prophecies," Silke answered.

THIRTY

W hile Suzanne told the story, Karn sat with his back against
a tree, listening. But when Wren glanced over at him, he
stood up.

"You're right. This story could be true. At least it's a better
explanation of the origin of the pendant. And what most of you
don't know is that there is another piece of 'jewelry' in play. Sawdi
found it years ago, slid it onto his finger, and I believe that it has
been controlling him ever since."

When no one said anything, he looked over at Suzanne and said,
"Bolong probably told you about it."

"Bolong?" Meg asked.

Suzanne's eyes filled with tears, shocking Meg, who went over to
sit beside her while Karn answered the question.

"Bolong is the head of the five dragons that make up the crown
of dragons controlled by Sawdi. Bolong and his friends are stuck
being dragons and can't shapeshift back to their true form. That
would have been my fate, too, if Wren hadn't rescued me from
Stryker's training camp."

Meg's heart almost broke when she looked at her sister and the
tears that threatened to overflow from her eyes. All these years,
thinking of nothing but how to help other people, and finally,
Suzanne had met someone she could love, and he could only be
a dragon? How could that be fair?

All Meg could think of was all the evil that Sawdi had done, and what he wanted to do with his Warrior Monks. She could feel the anger growing inside of her, and for a second, a flame licked out from her hand, causing Suzanne to flinch.

"Stop it," Karn yelled from across the clearing.

What felt like a steel lid slammed down inside Meg's brain, and the anger faded, to be replaced by despair. She had almost burned her sister.

"Stop that, too," Silke said as she hovered in front of Meg. "That kind of thinking makes you vulnerable to others controlling your thoughts.

"Which is what Aaron-Lem is all about. It controls your thinking. It takes over the ability to reason, imagine, be curious, or do anything other than follow the rules that Aaron, Stryker, and Sawdi have set up."

Suzanne turned to Meg and said, "I'm okay. Even if Bolong never returns to being a human, I can still love him. And yes, I do. It shocks me as much as it probably shocks you, Meg. I never expected to find a love that fit me, and I can only feel grateful that I have.

"It adds to my belief that we both came to Thamon for a reason. Maybe it was for both of us to find love. But I think it is also to bring the story of the brothers. Knowing who they were and what they did may help us defeat these three men and their followers. I am more determined than ever."

Turning to Karn, Suzanne said, "Yes. Bolong told me about Sawdi's ring. Do you think this is also part of something that the bored brothers brought to Thamon?"

When Karn nodded, Suzanne said, "It makes sense. Both of these items increase the temptation to have ultimate power and the need to control everyone and everything. Bolong told me that Sawdi has gotten much worse over the years. Perhaps you are right. The ring is the reason."

While the discussion was going on, Tarek had sat quietly watching. Finally, he turned to his father and asked, "Had you heard this story before, and that's one of the reasons you allowed Sawdi to capture you?"

Udore smiled at Tarek before answering. No matter what happened, Udore was grateful to be back with his son. He was so proud of him, and the wizard that he had become. Seeing him look at Meg made him happy, too. But of course, he had expected it.

"I had not heard the story the way Suzanne told it, but now that she has, it answers some of my questions about the prophecies. But I do have one more question for Suzanne. Did one brother bet that good would win, and one that evil would win? Was that the purpose of the experiment?"

"On Gaia, it was."

"Which answers why we have the prophecies. The brother who wanted good to win has given us clues as to how to stop the evil they had set into motion. The brother that wanted evil to win had the map made."

Meg thought for a moment and then said, "But didn't that make both brothers evil? Even the brother who wanted good to win went along with this terrible game that has caused so much suffering. So no matter what we do, isn't evil winning, because they forced us into this game?"

No one spoke. There was truth in Meg's words. But how were they to get around it?

"Well, from what I understand, on Erda, the brothers returned, but one of them realized what he had done was wrong," Suzanne said. "I don't know if the brothers ever came back here, but my guess is, although I have not read the prophesies, there is a clue or two in them on how to destroy both the pendant and the ring. Because isn't that what we have to do?"

"Yes, obviously, we do. But what about Aaron, Stryker, and Sawdi? What happens to them? Is that in those prophesies that you keep talking about?" Rose asked.

Silke and Wren looked at each other. Silke nodded at Wren, who then looked at Karn. It was Karn who answered, "What Silke and Wren aren't telling you is that the prophecies only hint at what happens to people involved with the pendant and ring. What it does tell us is that there would be someone who would be instrumental in the outcome."

When he turned to look at Meg, she croaked, "What? Why are you looking at me?"

"Haven't you figured it out yet, Meg?" Tarek asked, taking her hand.

Thirty One

"That's it?" Meg squeaked as everyone started standing and stretching, getting ready to travel.

"You can't just say that, and then not tell me more, Karn," Meg said, hands on her hips, staring at Karn and then Wren, Silke, and Tarek. "Obviously you have known about this, whatever you are talking about, but didn't share it with me.

"And now you are going to say something like that and leave? What am I supposed to do with that?"

"That's the point," Karn said. "If any of us tell you more, you will try to do something with it. So far, not knowing anything about it, you have done very well. If you try to control or direct what this looks like, it won't work, and you know that, don't you?"

Meg turned away, feeling like she did when she first came to Thamon, isolated and alone, and also ashamed of her behavior. She had been a wild-child who did what she wanted. She had been a shapeshifter who could be anything.

And now all of that was gone. Who was she now? Was she part of some prophecy, probably written thousands and thousands of years ago? What was she supposed to think about that?

Tarek reached out and pulled her close, wrapping his arms around her as Meg buried her face into his chest. Never in a million years had she ever thought she would find someone like Tarek, and be part of a community like the one she found herself in now. Karn was right, none of it had happened because of something she had made happen.

Tarek looked over Meg's head at Karn and nodded. She'd be okay. It was just a lot of information to take in. Tarek whispered to Meg that Leon was leaving, and she broke away and ran into Leon's arms.

"I'm so sorry, Leon, for thinking that being Ordinary was something bad or less. I was so wrong about so many things," Meg said, trying to keep from crying.

"Please be careful," she said, looking up at him.

"We will. And don't worry, child, we'll all be together again. And don't worry about the prophecies, and what you think you might have to do. You'll always do what is right. I saw that in you right away."

"How could you have seen that," Meg said. "I was, and probably still am such a brat."

Leon laughed his huge laugh and said, "Ah. It was only misdirected energy. Be a brat, Meg. You are brave, fearless, and loving, and I, for one, am better for knowing you."

"Aye," echoed the men standing with him.

Meg hugged each one, crying harder as she made her way around the circle. And then everyone was saying goodbye, hugging and crying as Leon and his men and the men from the Eos and Soleis slipped out into the woods, moving so quietly Meg couldn't hear them after they were gone a few feet.

Answering Meg's unspoken question of how they could be so quiet, Tarek said, "Leon is not as Ordinary as he claims. He is cloaking their sounds."

"He lied to me?"

"Not lied. Leon doesn't consider himself magical. It's a skill he has learned, like talking to me when we are far away from each other." Tarek smiled and then said, "Leon said to tell you that no one is Ordinary, but you have probably figured that out for yourself."

"What I have begun to see, Tarek, is that the word ordinary has no meaning. Everyone has gifts and skills. Sometimes they are called magic, and sometimes they are not."

"Exactly. That's what Leon said you would say."

Before Meg could answer, Karn called out. "Are we ready to move out, too?"

"Perhaps I have missed something?" Suzanne said. "Where are we going? Do you know where the pendant is?"

Karn looked at the group left in the clearing—Rose, Wren, Meg, Suzanne, Silke, Tarek, and Udore—and hoped that he was right. That they were the ones that could destroy the pendant. If not, all the plans that he and Udore had put into place would fail.

Karn nodded at Udore, who lifted his empty hand and waited. There was a small flash of light, and then something was in his hand.

"I don't, but this map does."

****

The room smelled musty and spicy at the same time. Stryker didn't like it. He had spent an unexpectedly restless night. He had thought being on stable ground and sleeping on a bed that didn't rock would ensure a good night's sleep.

The exact opposite had occurred. The stillness and the staleness of the air made him feel sick. First, the sea had made him sick, and now the dry land was doing the same thing? Would he ever feel like himself again?

Stryker missed his room back in the Temple on Hetale, which surprised him. He hadn't known that he would miss the Islands. Well, perhaps I can return there once I find the pendant, Stryker thought.

Maybe the pendant would give him another way there that didn't involve boats. Perhaps once he had all the power, he could take over Sawdi's crown of dragons and fly with them.

With that cheery thought, Stryker gave up trying to sleep and swung his legs onto the floor. He was sore all over, probably from bumping things while on the ship while it flung him from one side of the deck or his room to the other.

Despite not sleeping, or maybe because he hadn't, Stryker realized that he was hungry. The landlady said there would be food in the morning.

As he dressed, Stryker kept his eyes on the map that he had laid on the table the night before. He had hoped that it would show him where to go next and had not wanted to put it away, thinking that if he did, he might miss it.

As he turned to put on his cloak, Stryker thought he saw a flash of light coming from the map, but when he looked again, it was the same as before. There was nothing. It was blank. Sometimes he hated that map. Once again, it was playing with him, but Stryker didn't have a choice. It did what it wanted to, and he followed.

Thirty Two

D ax didn't leave right away, although he had wanted to. Keeping himself sane while he waited wasn't easy. But Ruth and Roar wanted to say goodbye to people and settle some of their affairs.

"You'd think they thought they weren't coming back," Dax complained to Ibris one morning.

They were sitting on Ibris' favorite bench, waiting for Etar and Trin to pass each other. Now that magic was once again allowed on the Islands, the ritual of stopping during the day for that moment had returned.

Ibris thought that it wasn't just the blue flash that people were looking for; it was the chance to pause during the day and enjoy whatever nature was offering up.

Every day the Islanders felt more and more the way they used to feel before the Kai-Via arrived. Although Dax was still not loved by the people, he had fully accepted that he never would be. Dax knew that the people tolerated him only because they knew what he was planning to do.

Of course, they were unhappy that their beloved Ruth and Roar would be going with him, but most of them understood that was the only way to get Dax there in time to stop Aaron from whatever he was planning next.

However, Dax and Ibris knew that there were people on the Islands that still worshiped Aaron, and they would be trying to get a message to Aaron that Dax was coming. But neither of them worried too much about that. How would they send a message? There had been no ships. No Mage would help them, and the Islands were cloaked, so unless you knew they were there, it would appear that the Warrior Monks and Sawdi had destroyed them.

But everyone knew that the Mages couldn't cloak the Islands forever, so sending Dax off to stop Aaron was something they fully endorsed. And no one besides Ibris really cared if Dax died in the process.

Even Ibris admitted to himself that perhaps it was the way that Dax would like to leave Thamon. He wondered if in death Dax might find a door to pass into a new life, one where Dax might find some peace. But that was all conjecture, and Ibris didn't want to lose his cousin. However, as deep as his faith was in redemption, Ibris knew it might be impossible for Dax to drop all his need for violence in this lifetime.

What worried Ibris was the Islander's desire for Dax to die along with Aaron. But then they knew that Ruth and Roar might die too, and no one wanted that. Most of all, Ibris didn't want Dax to be so cavalier about Ruth and Roar's support of his mission.

So his answer, "Of course they worry that they won't be coming back," was tinged with anger and bitterness.

Dax's retort was cut short by the blue flash and cheers from the crowd. As much as Dax didn't want to admit it, he was hoping for that blue flash. Even for him, it was a symbol of hope for what he had to do.

Although he had long ago accepted that someday he would have to die, Dax didn't believe the way Ibris did that there were more lives after death, that death was simply a transition.

To Dax, death was a closed door. It was over. No punishment, no reward. He supposed that if he was wrong, he might be angry at himself for some of his choices.

Maybe that was another reason he was going after Aaron to stop him. If he was wrong, and there was an accounting system in place, perhaps this act would be one check mark on the right side.

There had been a time in his life when Dax had thought that perhaps there was a God who did control the universes. He had even entertained the idea that it was a good God, not one of vengeance. But after his family was killed, he stopped believing that.

Why them? Why did his parents have to die? His parents believed in good. They believed that good people thrived. And then look what happened to them. They were killed so that a power hungry fake god who ruled with greed could get him, Dax, and train him to be Kai-Via.

Aaron, Stryker, and Sawdi had destroyed hundreds of good people to get to one person. The one person who didn't deserve it. And then they made that one person become as evil as them. The small thing Dax could do now would never make up for what he had done in the past. But perhaps he could stop at least one of them.

He could do something for the one remaining person from his family who loved him in spite of it all. For a second, it gave him hope that what Ibris believed was right, that there was a good God.

Ibris put his arm around his cousin Dax knowing what he was thinking. Dax was right. He did still love him. And he believed in him, despite all his horrendous acts.

After all, Ibris thought, I was the Preacher of Aaron-Lem. What makes me better than him? Perhaps together, we can make up for what we allowed and assisted in some ways to happen.

That's the way Ruth and Roar found them. Sitting on the bench. Ibris, with his arm around Dax, watching the ocean together.

Ruth and Roar had seen the blue flash too, while standing on the Arrow, saying goodbye to friends.

127

After the flash, it was Roar who said, "We could put this off forever, Ruth. But it is time to go."

Ruth nodded, hugged the shop keeper who had just gifted her with a beautiful new cloak, and turned towards Hetale. As they reached the end of the Arrow, they heard someone yell, "Hey," and Ruth and Roar turned around to see everyone who had been at the market waving to them.

"Be safe! Come back!" they were saying.

Ruth burst into tears and reached for Roar's hand. They bowed to the crowd and then turned to the beach, both of them not sure if they would ever return. Both of them thinking they wouldn't.

THIRTY THREE

They had been at the cabin for a few days, and Bolong was almost tired of waiting. It was the thought of what would probably come next that kept him quiet.

Sawdi had jumped off Bolong without saying a word, had gone inside the cabin, and hadn't come out again. Of course, Sawdi had not done anything to take care of his dragon. Bolong wondered if it ever occurred to Sawdi that the dragon he rode everywhere also needed food.

Luckily, there was plenty of fresh grass and young leaves for him to eat. He found the bed he had made out of moss the last few times they had visited and settled down under the bush that covered his lair to wait it out.

In some ways, Bolong was happy that it was just him with Sawdi, that Sawdi had not gone back to the Palace right away. It gave him time to think about what had happened to him. It was something he had never believed possible. So impossible, he had never allowed himself to even dream about it. Without warning, without a hint that it was coming, he had found love.

Bolong thought back to the moment he had watched a beautiful dragon, with a red streak like him, land, and then shift into a beautiful woman. He had been so shocked at the sight that he almost roared and shot out a tongue of fire by mistake.

After they learned who she was, the entire crown had rejoiced. Her presence not only meant that there were other dragons on

Thamon, but that there was a rebellion in place. Even if they were never able to return to being men, there was the chance that they could be free.

Leaving the Islands that day, Bolong had worried that Suzanne would not be able to make the trip to the Palace while he and the rest of the dragons returned out of time with Sawdi. He fretted and barely slept while he waited. His friends teased him. But they were just as worried. Perhaps Suzanne was not the love of their life, the way she was for him, but she was their touchstone to the rebellion.

The night she had crept into their den, they rejoiced. She was exhausted. They had prepared a hidden bed for her at the back of their cave in case Sawdi ever decided to step into their cave instead of standing outside and demanding attention.

It was a few days before Suzanne fully regained her strength and started the work that she had come to do. She began walking out into Edes, looking for others who were part of the resistance. Karn had supplied her with a list. She would be gone all day, but at night she returned, and she and Bolong had talked for hours.

She had told him all about her life before. Suzanne told stories of her life in the Earth Realm as an ambassador from Erda. She had described her sister and said that this was the first time she wished she could be more than one thing, the way that Meg could. It would make her work on Edes more manageable.

As it was, she had changed her appearance as much as possible. Karn had left her a cache of clothes that the women of Edes wore, and that had helped. The hardest part had been getting into the prison.

But one of the guards was part of the resistance, and he had smuggled her in so she and Udore could make plans.

It amazed Bolong how many people were already part of the rebellion, but were waiting for the right time to take action. When Bolong asked Suzanne if she knew when that time would be, she had replied that everyone would know when it was the time.

For now, they would stay quiet and do what needed to be done to be ready. Bolong wasn't surprised to hear that it had been Karn who was behind much of the planning. What he was upset about was why Karn had not come to see him before he left the Palace.

Suzanne said it had been in case Sawdi could read Bolong's thoughts. Karn pretending to be one of the blind Blessed Ones had been hard enough. As Bolong lay on the moss waiting for Sawdi to return, he smiled to himself.

While Stryker had been training his "boys" to be warriors, Kai-Via, and Preachers, there had always been a rebellion fighting him, right under his nose, which included Bolong, his four friends, Falcon, and Karn. Stryker may have trained them, but they would use that training to defeat him, Aaron, and Sawdi.

Bolong wasn't sure if he was happy or sad to see Sawdi open the cabin door and call to him. He assumed that they would be going back to the Palace. And he hated it when the Warrior Monks were there.

As Sawdi climbed onto his back, Bolong noticed that he strained to get there. Did he appear thinner, tired, and weaker? Perhaps it would be easier to defeat him in this state. But Bolong stopped that thinking immediately.

As Karn had said, it was possible Sawdi could tap into his thoughts. But that wasn't the only reason he stopped himself. He had seen the ring glowing, and Bolong suspected that it was the ring that was draining Sawdi. That wasn't good news. It just meant that the ring had gotten stronger.

Before leaving, Suzanne had shared the story of the two bored brothers who had experimented with planets because they didn't know what else to do with themselves. She speculated that it was the brothers who had placed the pendant and ring on Thamon as a test of good against evil.

If that was the case, they had to discover how to defeat not only the people involved, but to destroy the pendant and ring. Suzanne was confident that they could. She had said, "If someone gave them power, we can take it back." But the answer to how to do that was still a mystery.

Bolong sighed as he saw the Palace in the distance. Suzanne had told him very little about what the resistance was planning. The fact that Udore was gone, and Aaron's secret lair of women and children had been rescued, told him that the plan was working.

All he knew is that whatever they asked of him, he was willing to do. He just hoped that it meant at the end of it all, he would be with Suzanne. Even as a dragon. Bolong smiled to himself and swooped around the Palace. Even the sight of the Warrior Monks swirling like a gluttonous mass below him didn't dampen his spirits.

Sawdi tensed. Beneath him, Bolong felt different. What was it? Perhaps he was just happy to be flying again. He had stayed too long at the cabin. For some reason, instead of reviving him, the visit had drained him. But the ring had plans, and Sawdi could no longer even dream of resisting it.

THIRTY FOUR

L ike Stryker's map, the map that Udore had pulled out of thin air remained blank. The only way they knew it was a map was Udore had told them it was, and the seven people watching him had to believe him.

After all, they had nothing else to guide them. Not that a blank map was much help. All questions about how Udore had gotten the map were brushed aside by Udore. There were only a few that he would answer. "No, he hadn't taken Stryker's map. He pulled out a copy. No, Stryker would not know."

To the question of why it was blank, he answered, "Because this map plays tricks. Stryker's map was blank when I pulled the copy, so this one is too. When Stryker's map shows him where the next piece is, so will this one."

"But how do we get there first?" Meg asked, almost afraid to say anything. After all, this was Tarek's father and a powerful wizard.

"Why don't we have Joseph and Fionn steal his map and hide it? Or destroy it. Oh, maybe not destroy it because then maybe this map won't work. But wait. If you can pull a copy, why didn't you just take the real thing?"

Realizing what she had said to Udore, she added, "Sir."

Udore laughed and shrugged. "You're right, of course. That would be so much easier. I have stolen this map before, just the way you suggested. It would come into my hand, and then it would disappear. Eventually, I realized that it was attached to Stryker, and no one can steal it.

"I couldn't even copy it before. This is the first time I tried it that it worked."

"Why did it work now?" Meg asked.

"We are back to the prophesies, Meg," Udore said, glancing over at Karn.

Meg felt her temper flare again. But when Silke landed on her shoulder, she was able to tap it back down.

"Is it going to do any good to ask you what you mean, or are you going to hide all of it from me."

Karn answered her. "We aren't hiding it, Meg. We are simply not telling you right now. You, like us, will have to trust that if we do our part, we have a chance.

"If we don't, then it won't matter, because what Stryker doesn't know is that putting the pendant together might not work out the way he thinks it will.

"If the ring and the pendant are in the same place at the same time without being destroyed, then there won't be a planet to save."

"You mean the bored brothers would have gone that far? They would have put a full destruction in place?" Rose asked. "How could they have thought that would be okay?"

"Well, at least one of them must have hoped it didn't happen. But it would be the ultimate test if good can win over evil," Suzanne said.

"In Erda, did good win?" Tarek asked.

"It did," Suzanne answered, "And I trust that will be true here."

"So say we all," the eight of them said together.

Suzanne recognized that saying from her time in the Earth Realm, and was happy to hear it again on this strange planet. Of course, that begged the question of how everyone knew it. But it was not something she was planning to waste time thinking about for now. They had much bigger issues to deal with, and so few answers to help them.

****

It was the first food that Stryker had eaten that tasted good to him since he had left the Islands. The landlady was right. She was a good cook. Or maybe it was because he wasn't sick anymore.

He was beginning to suspect that Captain Kosti had done something that kept the ship rocking all the time, probably to keep him seasick. But Stryker couldn't prove it, and Kosti was long gone.

However, once he was the ruler of the planet, perhaps he would spend a little time tracking him down and extracting the truth from him.

But first the map. Stryker knew that Sawdi would figure out where he was going, and would eventually come after him. Why he hadn't already didn't mean that he didn't know where Stryker had gone, but only that he was biding his time. Sawdi would wait for the perfect moment, and only Sawdi would know when that time was.

Since no one in Yeal Thalor knew who he was, Stryker didn't worry about hiding himself, or the map. It was the first time since they had started Aaron-Lem that Stryker felt free. He found that a strange feeling. Shouldn't he have felt free before?

A bell rang in the distance, and everyone stopped what they were doing and turned towards the east.

What's going on? Stryker asked himself.

When he realized what was happening, he couldn't believe it. Even here, in this tiny remote village on Turva, the people were getting ready to pray to Aaron.

Stryker followed the lead of everyone around him. Through the window, he could see that everyone, even those outside on the street, was bowing.

As he bent his forehead to the floor, Stryker couldn't stop smiling. They had done it. They had brought the whole of Thamon under their rule. As much as they had dreamed of it happening, all the long nights together talking about how they were going to do it, here it was. Done.

That's when it occurred to him that perhaps there were people in Yeal Thalor who might recognize him. If they were bowing, maybe then there were Kai-Via and a Preacher in town. He couldn't keep track of all of them all over Thamon.

What if they were here, and one of them was someone he had trained? Perhaps they could help him stop Sawdi when he arrived. He wouldn't be alone after all.

As the bell rang again, releasing them from bowing, Stryker looked around the room. Standing along the wall, looking his way, was someone that Stryker recognized. Yes, the Kai-Via was here. How could he use them to stop Sawdi while he looked for the pendant?

What Stryker didn't see were the two men watching him. They, too, saw the man leaning against the wall. Watching Stryker's reaction, they knew who it must be. But what Stryker didn't realize was that Karn had recruited members of the Kai-Via, and some Preachers, to be part of the resistance.

What they needed to find out was which side this man was on, before Stryker did.

Thirty Five

Before leaving the Islands, Dax did one last thing. Something only he could do, because he was the only one who knew about it. Dax freed the women. At first, he was just going to unlock the door of the small cabin where they had lived the last year. But then he started worrying about their survival.

They knew no one but him on the Islands. How would they explain who they were? Would they be accepted? Besides, they were blind. How would they fend for themselves?

Dax always knew that eventually, he would let them go. He had rarely used them. Yes, even though those words made his skin crawl. They were the words that Aaron had used when he had gifted the two women to Dax before he had left for the Islands.

Dax had tried to refuse, but Aaron would not take no for an answer. Aaron had walked through the rooms filled with the women of the Blessed Ones and handpicked the two for Dax.

"Take two," he had said, as if what he was offering were pieces of candy. "You know, in case one of them dies on the way," he added.

Seeing that he had no choice, Dax had led them away, and for the most part, stayed away from them except to make sure they had food and clothes when he remembered them. Since no one was supposed to know about the women of the Blessed Ones, he couldn't have anyone but himself look after them, which he didn't do well.

And now he wanted to set them free. Otherwise, they would die in that little house. He didn't want to travel to Aaron's to kill him with anything he regretted left on his soul. Whatever a soul was, Dax wanted to feel as if he had one. Just in case there was a real god.

But he still couldn't bring himself to admit what he had allowed himself to be part of. Killing and violence was one thing. Treating women like things was not the same for him. It was a small distinction in his mind, but big enough for him to finally decide to tell Samis about the women.

Dax thought that of all the people he knew, Samis would be the one who could help the women be welcomed into the Islands' community of people. He and his little band of rebels had stayed under the radar all this time. They would have resources to help the women.

But Dax didn't tell Samis why they were taking a path into the woods on Hetale where he had never been before. Samis was on alert. Was Dax going to betray them all, and kill Samis first? But watching Dax let branches slap him in the face and stumble over rocks he would have customarily stepped over, Samis lost his fear.

Something was wrong, but it wasn't that Dax was getting ready to kill him. After a twenty-minute walk, Dax ducked under two low hanging branches of a pine tree. Samis followed and found a small path that twisted around the stand of pine trees and then opened up to reveal a cabin set among the trees. Dax was already at the front door, unlocking it before Samis had recovered from seeing a cabin in the middle of the woods.

Dax waited for Samis to catch up before pushing the door open the whole way. The tiny cabin was completely dark. It was only the weak beam of sunlight that came through the open door that enabled Samis to see the two women sitting together on the floor, hugging each other, terror showing through the dirt on their faces.

"What the zonk is going on here?" Samis hissed, but then stopped when he saw the women drawback in fear from his words.

Samis grabbed Dax and pulled him outside. "Who are those women, Dax? Why are they here? What have you done to them?"

Responding to Samis' anger, Dax stepped closer to Samis and hissed into his face, "I never hurt them. No, I didn't take care of them. But I didn't hurt them."

Stepping back, he handed Samis the keys to the cabin and told him in a few brief sentences who the women were and why they were there, then turned and walked out of the woods, leaving Samis wondering how the world could have gotten so sick.

Samis stepped back into the cabin and bent down so that he was level with the women. Dax had told him that they were blind, and now he understood why the cabin was dark. As gently as he could, Samis told them who he was.

He explained that they were free now, and that he had friends who would help. Women friends. He wanted to add the words "like you," but he knew that would never be true. Who they were and what happened to them would never be something someone else could understand.

When the women didn't answer, Samis sat down at the opening of the door and waited. Finally, one of the women whispered, "Free?"

"Free," Samis answered. "If you come with me, I'll take you to town and find you a real home."

It would be many months before the women told the full story of their life with Aaron at his Palace and then in the cabin mostly ignored by Dax. By then, everyone knew what Aaron had been trying to do.

Dax walked away from the cabin as quickly as he could. He told himself that he had done the right thing. He wanted to do the right thing. And that's what he wanted to do now. Do at least one big right thing, the action that would set all the world free from Aaron.

Ruth and Roar were waiting for Dax on the shore of Hetale. Dax wasn't surprised to see Ibris there too. Ibris was the best friend he ever had. Ibris had held Dax in his heart as his spiritual brother. Perhaps what he would do at the Palace would make up for the times he had forgotten that.

At the very least, he would be using his gifts of violence and killing to do something good. If that counted for anything, Dax didn't know.

Roar shifted into a dragon and lay as flat as he could in the sand so that Ruth could clamber on, mumbling under her breath that she couldn't believe that Roar had been a dragon all this time, and he had been her best friend and never told her, and this whole thing was crazy.

Roar let out a little flame of fire, laughing at Ruth's ranting, and then Dax climbed up and put his arms around Ruth. She flinched and then steeled herself. They all had a job to do. This was no time to have a division between them.

Within seconds, the three of them were invisible to Ibris, who stayed on the shore, trying not to cry. He didn't think he would ever see Dax again, and he could only pray that Ruth and Roar would return.

Ibris turned and saw Oiseon waiting for him on the cliff. Ibris knew what Oiseon was trying to tell him. They had two islands full of people that needed their care and attention.

Ibris sighed, used the tail of his cloak to wipe his eyes, and headed back towards the people who needed him. After all that he had been part of, it was the least that he could do.

THIRTY SIX

No one had time to ask any more questions. The map had blinked on. The seven people in the woods were the first to see it.

Stryker was busy and missed it. He was following the man who had been leaning up against the wall. And Joseph and Fionn were following Stryker.

It was apparent that the man they were all following either didn't know he was being followed or didn't care. The man walked straight through the town and towards a building at the end of the main street. Yeal Thalor was so small it only had one main road, so it would have been hard to hide where he was going, anyway.

Once the man went into the building, Stryker stopped in the middle of the road and started laughing. He laughed so hard he was bent over with his hands on his knees, trying to catch his breath. No one looked his way, which confused Joseph and Fionn.

Did the people know who Stryker was and were afraid of him? Or did they always ignore strangers laughing like a crazy person in the middle of the street?

To add to the strangeness, no one looked at them either. Here they were, two strangers, standing in the shadows of a building watching the street. Wouldn't people be curious about why?

"What is going on? Are they afraid of someone?" Joseph whispered to Fionn.

"Or something," Fionn whispered back. "The question is, what is Stryker laughing about?"

They waited until Stryker turned and went back to the boarding house before they ventured out into the street. Sure, no one appeared as if they were watching them, but what if they were? On the other hand, what was wrong with walking down a street to a building?

As they got closer, they saw what Stryker had seen. Above the door of the tiny, nondescript, off white building, were the words, The Temple.

Both of them almost did the same thing that Stryker had just done. This was the Temple? This building was a joke. The whole thing could fit into one of the rooms of the Temple on the Islands.

But they both restrained themselves. Taking a minute to prepare themselves to look like one of the Converted, Joseph and Fionn reverently opened the door and stepped inside.

The man Stryker had been following was at the front of the room, leaning against the pulpit, facing the door.

"I wondered which of you would come inside," he said. "I am glad it was you. Would you follow me, please?"

When Joseph and Fionn stayed where they were, he said, "Seriously, don't just stand there. Would it help if I told you that I am a friend of Karn and Falcon?

"Oh, and by the way, your friend, that wren sitting outside on the tree, would like to come inside too."

****

"You were expecting us?" Wren asked after everyone had followed the man into a room located at the back of the building, not much bigger than a closet.

"Well, not specifically you. The prophecies are not that specific. And Karn wasn't sure who would come. Although, I do have to say he has done a great job of planning so far."

The man smiled at Wren. "And I have to say he did a fairly good job of describing you, Wren."

Wren forced herself to not visibly bristle at this stranger's casual ways. She reminded herself that she was the elder here, by more than a few hundred years, although this man seemed to know things that she didn't, and that did make her a tiny bit angry. Not at the man. At Karn.

Once again, her crazy husband had kept things from her. For so many years, she had tried to get Karn out of her mind. Thinking he had abandoned her, betrayed her even. Then he showed up and helped save them all, and had been planning a large scale rebellion for years, and never told her.

All that passed through Wren's mind in the split second it took her to rearrange her face to be more accepting, despite wanting to spit.

So she calmly and sweetly said, "Oh yes, that Karn. He is quite the character and planner."

"But I am afraid he never got around to telling me about you. And if you please, could we start with your name, and why you are here.

"Are you the Preacher here or one of the Kai-Via? And while you are at it, how did you meet Karn? And oh, a side note, what is the plan that you know about?"

The man laughed, and when he did, Wren looked again. He reminded her of someone. He reminded her of Ibris, with an attitude.

"Show who you are, right now," Wren demanded.

Joseph and Fionn looked at Wren and then back to the man, who shrugged his shoulders and then shifted. Not much. Just enough to see his true age. And who he was. Standing before her was an older version of Ibris.

"Yes," the man said, "I am Ian Rissanen, Ibris' father, and Udore's brother."

A second later, Udore was in the room, and Ian and Udore were hugging and slapping each other on the back.

Wren stood with her arms crossed. "Udore, did you know Ian was here?"

Udore turned to Wren and held out his hand, palm down. "Wren, calm down. I am not really keeping things from you or the rest of our group. I wasn't sure Ian had survived. Yes, this was the plan.

"Ian was to come here, and take over the Temple, make it look as if the Kai-Via is thriving here. But I didn't know he did it until I heard him say his name."

Wren sat. "How deep does this plan go? Who else is in on it?"

"Not here," Ian said. "I'll come to the woods tonight, and we'll talk. Stryker is on his way here now. You'd best go."

Ian pointed to the two men and said, "Go out the back door. You don't need to stay in town right now. I'll watch Stryker."

One last hug and Udore was gone, leaving only Wren with Ian. "Does Ibris know?"

Ian shook his head while shifting back to a younger man. "No. And neither does Rose. Would you let me tell her when I get there tonight?"

Wren nodded and said, "Of course," flying out the open back door, just as Stryker entered the Temple. She heard Ian welcome him as if he didn't know who he was.

Wren said a silent prayer for Ian's safety and followed Joseph and Fionn back to the woods.

THIRTY SEVEN

When the map came on, everyone crowded around it, trying to see what it was telling them. Udore had just started to point out something on the map when he blinked away, and the map went with him.

Tarek, Silke, Suzanne, Meg, Karn, and Rose stared in horror at where he and the map had gone. Did the map do something to him? Did Stryker discover Udore and whisk him away? Not that Stryker had those kinds of powers, but that and multiple other scenarios went through their minds in the seconds before Udore was back, smiling, and holding the map. His smiling was almost as big a shock as his leaving. Finally, Tarek cleared his throat and said, "Would you mind telling us what just happened?"

And Rose added, "And don't do it again either, that is, if you have a choice. That scared the ziffer out of me."

Udore smiled at his son and his niece and said, "I'm sorry. I was just so shocked to..." and then, realizing what he was about to say, stopped himself.

Ian had asked him not to tell. So Udore stumbled through a few words which meant nothing, and then said, "Shall we look at this map now?"

Everyone stared at Udore, not believing anything he had said, but also curious about the map. So they let it go. Silke whispered in Suzanne's ear, "Something's up."

Suzanne nodded and then whispered back, "But it must be good because otherwise, why was he smiling?"

Udore wasn't smiling anymore. His attention was on the map. "Look, Karn," he said. "Does this mean what I think it does?"

Karn took the map from Udore and sighed. "I hate and love this map. It shows something and then takes it away. But at the moment, it is giving us some direction. And you're right, that is a path. When do you want to start?"

"In the morning. We need to wait for Wren to return. But let's move closer to the mountain. Wren will find us, and we'll have a head start."

"Head start where?" Suzanne asked.

"Up the mountain," Karn answered. "It's not going to be an easy trip. But we have a head start on Stryker. Even if he saw the map at the same time we did, he will need to get provisions. He'll be behind us."

Meg wanted to scream in irritation. Everyone was talking so calmly, as if there wasn't a monster called Stryker only miles away from them, and another one coming with those white wraiths sooner or later. What could they possibly be waiting for that was keeping them here?

But instead of screaming, she helped pack up and followed Udore and Karn towards the mountain.

After walking an hour or so, and then setting up a new camp, Wren arrived. She hugged Karn and looked as if she was going to burst apart with a secret. She and Karn exchanged looks, and Wren shook her head when he started to ask her a question.

Meg heard her whisper, "Yes. He'll be here," and then walked over to talk to Udore.

The only thing that kept Meg from punching Karn in the arm to get him to tell her what was going on was that neither he nor Wren seemed to be worried. So that must mean that whatever was happening had to be good? And, of course, everyone else was busy setting up camp and acting as if nothing different was happening.

An hour or so later, Joseph and Fionn came into the camp. Once again, hugs were exchanged, and to Meg's frustration, no one seemed to notice that they were no longer watching Stryker.

Meg watched Udore walk over to Rose and put his arm around her. Why? Meg asked herself. A second later there was a now-familiar flash, and someone else was standing in front of Udore and Rose.

Rose gasped, and asked so quietly that Meg could barely hear her, "Dad?"

The man shifted, and Rose screamed and fell into his arms.

Meg watched the two of them hugging, the man with tears running down his face, and Rose sobbing, and then Tarek walked over and put his arm around them both.

"What is happening, Silke?" Meg asked the Okan who had landed on her shoulder, probably knowing that Meg would want and need answers.

"Well, I think it's pretty obvious. That's Rose's father, Ian, and of course, Udore's brother and Tarek's uncle."

Meg stamped her foot. "Of course, I see that. He looks like Ibris. But where did he come from? I thought he was dead."

"Well, everyone did, except maybe Karn."

Meg looked over at Karn, standing a few feet away, holding hands with Wren. He glanced her way and winked.

Meg was beginning to understand why Wren had gotten frustrated with Karn. Did he ever tell all that was going on? Was Karn always about secrets? What wasn't he telling them? And that string of thoughts brought her back to wondering about herself. Why wouldn't he tell her what she was supposed to do?

Watching people shift, or blink away and back, and feeling completely in the dark and inadequate was starting to get to her. Even Suzanne was still able to be a dragon. But other than feeling as if a fire was burning inside of her when she got too angry, Meg could do nothing else. The ability to shift into anything she wanted to be was gone.

And that fire burning inside was not that good a thing, anyway. It was dangerous. Meg didn't know if she could contain it. And without Karn, would she be able to keep from burning herself up if it surrounded her again?

Meg turned away, feeling ashamed again that she was still only thinking of herself, and walked into the woods. Let them have their celebration. She didn't belong there. She was an outsider.

Meg almost screamed out loud when she heard a voice beside her say, "Those are the kind of thoughts that can destroy you and your friends."

Meg turned to look, and the man they said was Ian was standing beside her.

"Don't you have better things to do than follow a stranger into the woods?" Meg snapped back.

"Not a stranger, Meg," Ian replied.

THIRTY EIGHT

Sawdi made Bolong circle the Palace. Over and over again. First, they would dip down as if they were going to land, and then Sawdi would pull Bolong up, and they would circle again.

Bolong was afraid to think too much about it, in case Sawdi probed into his thoughts. As far as Sawdi was concerned, Bolong and his crown of dragons had very little ability to think for themselves, and they wanted to keep it that way.

But Bolong allowed himself to be a little curious because Sawdi would expect him to wonder what they were doing.

Below them, the landscape was as desolate as always, or had become since Aaron had taken over the land. Aaron wanted his Palace to shine out like a beacon, and that it did. All the gold and gemstones lining the windows and doors shot out rays of light, alerting everyone that their God lived there.

Except now. Now those rays of sparkling light were absorbed by the mass of Warrior Monks who had settled in the courtyard, covering every inch of it with a white writhing mass.

Even flying as high as he was, Bolong could hear the low hum as if there were thousands of angry bees below them. It was just loud enough to be threatening, and soft enough to seep into the skin and memory and stay there. Bolong knew his friends were probably trying to ignore it, trying to rest. But even though they didn't live on the Palace grounds, they would still hear it. The sound would vibrate through the earth and up into their bodies, causing nightmares and anxiety, just as Sawdi intended.

About the tenth time around, Bolong spotted a person hiding behind one of the spires on the Palace roof so well hidden that only a dragon would have seen him. A person who knew that dragons had eyesight far superior to humans, or even wizards. Even Sawdi.

Bolong knew who it was, and he knew Baywolf was there for him because he rarely showed himself unless it was urgent. He was Aaron's secret. Or so Aaron thought.

As Sawdi had Bolong dip lower, perhaps intending to land this time, Bolong could see that Baywolf was pointing towards the crown's cave.

He's trying to tell me someone is in the den, Bolong realized, and then stopped thinking about it. Bolong suspected that whoever was in the cave was probably friendly because Baywolf didn't give off any signs of fear. He was only telling Bolong to be aware so that he didn't overreact when he saw them.

As they circled lower, Bolong realized that Sawdi was planning to have him land on the roof of the Palace, and for that, he was grateful. He had no desire to land in the middle of the Warrior Monks. Because once the Monks realized that Sawdi was landing, they had started that horrible howling.

It was their happy sound. They made it only when they killed, and when they saw Sawdi. As the howling increased, Bolong touched down. He looked for Baywolf but didn't see him.

As Bolong flattened himself to the ground so that he could quickly dismount, Sawdi said, "We'll be leaving in the morning."

Bolong knew that Sawdi could have added, "That means you need to get rest and food. I don't want you to be tired and useless." But he didn't.

Instead, he flipped his cloak behind him, walked to the edge of the roof, waved his arms at the Warrior Monks below, nodded to the increased howling, and then waited until one separated himself and drifted up until he, or it, was level with Sawdi's face.

They stared at each other for what felt like hours to Bolong, who tried not to quiver at the increased howling and what he saw happen between Sawdi and the Monk. Finally, the Monk drifted back down to the mass below him.

Sawdi turned and noticing that Bolong was still on the roof with him, and shrieked, "Go, now!"

Bolong bowed his head, turned, and lifted off to go back to the crown's den in the cave. Below him, Sawdi stood, his hands clenched. Bolong knew he was not supposed to see what he had seen. If Sawdi was worried about him before, he had just made it worse.

It didn't matter. Bolong knew that Sawdi's plans included eliminating him and his friends sooner or later. Perhaps the later had arrived. But he had a little time. Sawdi would need a ride in the morning, and Bolong was the only one who could take him.

Whether or not he planned to let him return to the Palace was questionable. But Bolong didn't care about that. Whatever happened, none of them expected to return to the Palace.

Even so, Bolong hoped that whoever was at the den with his friends was someone that could help.

Sawdi watched Bolong lift away and shivered. He wasn't cold. He was afraid, angry, and worried. But it wasn't any of those emotions that made him shiver. It was fear. He was terrified of the ring.

It was the ring that had called the Warrior Monk, not him. Even though Sawdi knew it was the ring, it was hard to accept. He had always considered himself wise, powerful, and willing to do whatever it took to be in control. But now, the ring was letting him know that he had lost that ability. The ring had taken his power away bit by bit, starting with the moment he had slid it onto his finger.

Sawdi didn't know if there had ever been a time that he was in charge and not the ring. Perhaps, in the beginning, he could have taken the ring off. But it was useless to think about it. It couldn't happen now.

What worried Sawdi was that Bolong had seen what the ring had done. When the ring called the Warrior Monk, the Monk's eyes had glowed the same as the ring. A piercing red beam had passed between them. For that moment, it was as if they were one thing.

Sawdi wondered how long the ring would need him. He knew that Bolong's days were numbered, but what about his?

What neither the ring or Sawdi saw was one green eye peering through a hole in the wall of one of the spires. Neither knew that it was hollow. No one did—except the man standing inside the small space.

Baywolf had also seen what the ring had done, and he knew what it meant. Time was running out for all of them. It was time to do what he had been planning for years.

Thirty Nine

D ax almost threw up at the smell. Good gods, he had no idea that dragons could smell that bad. He supposed that it was because they were stuck in that dark cave and had nowhere else to be, but he didn't know how he would be able to stay there with them.

Somehow Roar had known where the other dragons were staying and brought them down outside the cave, and then shifted back into a man. The four dragons in the cave turned and looked at them without expression. Dax thought they would have been more surprised to see them, but instead, they had moved to the front of the cave and been there ever since. Staring.

Every once in a while, one or two of them would huff out a puff of steam, which made Dax want to run. But Roar had assured Dax that they were friendly. Suzanne had met them when they were on the Islands and made friends with them. On the other hand, maybe it was because they were dragons, and they knew that they had the upper hand?

Dax had stepped back and stared at Roar and Ruth as if he had never seen them before. Perhaps he hadn't. Suzanne? Did he know a Suzanne? And she was a dragon too? Where was she now? How much had happened on the Islands right underneath his nose?

All along, Dax had thought that he had control of the Islands. It had been hard enough when he discovered that the Mages and shapeshifters that he thought he had killed were still alive. But this? How was he supposed to deal with all of this?

Dax wasn't sure what to do. All that he had thought that he was had been slowly crumbling away, and this was just one more thing he hadn't known. Seeing Dax's distress, Ruth and Roar assured Dax that he had glimpsed Suzanne at least once, but perhaps hadn't grasped who she was and why she was there.

As for his question about where Suzanne was now, Ruth and Roar didn't know, and the dragons in the cave weren't talking. The dragons staring at him scared the ziffer out of Dax. He was reasonably sure that if Ruth and Roar weren't standing in front of him, and that Roar was also a dragon—sometimes—they would have fried him right then and there.

After a few minutes of waiting for a response and not getting one, Ruth suggested that they rest. Obviously, the four dragons were waiting for their leader, Bolong, before deciding what to do with them.

Dax reluctantly agreed. It was hard to believe how tired the trip had made him. Ruth had explained that even though they had arrived quickly traveling out of time, their bodies thought that all the time had passed. So resting was a good thing.

The three of them moved away from the cave, for which Dax was grateful, and settled down next to an outcropping far enough away for the smell to be less noticeable, but not so far away that they couldn't see the cave opening. Roar closed his eyes and fell immediately to sleep.

"He is the most exhausted," Ruth explained. "He did all the work. We just rode along."

Dax stared at Ruth and, being too tired to stop himself, he said, "I understand why you are helping me. You want to stop Aaron too, but I don't understand why you don't hate me."

Ruth adjusted herself so that she was facing Dax before answering. "Would you prefer that I did?"

"I would understand that," Dax replied. "I hate all the time."

"Including what you have done, and seem to have become?" Ruth asked.

"Mostly that," Dax said. "Was I always this person that found it easy to kill, or need to kill, or desire to be violent?

"Why would Ibris still love me, because I know he does? And why are you kind to me? Maybe if I could understand why you don't hate, I would feel better. I know it's hate that is eating me up, and perhaps you are wiser than me. But kindness? Why are you kind to me?"

Ruth reached out and patted Dax's hand. "It's harder to hate than to be kind, Dax. But kindness is something we have to practice.

"And I have a feeling that, other than Ibris, you haven't been treated kindly for a long time. However, you recognize kindness, and although you might not understand why, you appreciate it.

"In my experience," Ruth continued, "Being able to recognize and appreciate kindness means that somewhere deep inside of you, you have that ability too."

Dax snorted and pulled his hands back as if they had betrayed him. "Me, kind? I don't think so. All I can think about is killing Aaron. Where's the kindness in that?"

"Dax, I was there when you told us all that you couldn't stop your violent thoughts, and instead of unleashing it on the people on the Islands, you wanted to come here to stop Aaron."

Dax nodded, confused about what she was telling him.

"That was an act of kindness, Dax. You wanted to save people, yes from yourself, but still, you were being kind, in your own way.

"That's why we are here to help you. You want to do the right thing. Yes, you didn't do the right thing before, but I do believe that once we discover we are not our impulses, we begin to have a handle on our true nature and act from that more often. I think you are doing that, Dax. And, as I said, it takes practice."

Dax looked away. His emotions were going crazy. I must be exhausted, he thought. But Ruth's words had somehow seeped into a crack in his heart that he didn't know was there. Was he really not this violent, power-crazed person? Did he have a spark of something else left in him? What would his parents think of him now?

"Your parents would be proud of you," Ruth whispered.

"How do you know?" Dax said, his face still turned away from her. There was no way he was going to let her see that his eyes were filled with tears.

"Because I am," Ruth said, "And I am a parent. Now go to sleep."

Ruth reached over and took one of Dax's hands, and surprising himself, Dax let her.

And that's how Bolong found them. Three sleeping humans, and four dragons guarding the cave, and he smiled to himself. They had come to help.

He even knew one of them. That he was letting that woman hold his hand surprised him. But things were changing, and he was happy to see Dax. Karn had said that if Dax decided to help, they might have a chance. He hoped Karn was right. So far, he had been.

FORTY

Sawdi had to decide. Take the Warrior Monks or leave them behind. He knew he was fooling himself. He wasn't the one who was doing the choosing. It was the ring.

His hand felt as if it was on fire. But Sawdi knew that he couldn't let anyone know that it was the ring that was in charge. Eventually, he would find a way to defeat the ring. For his sake, he hoped sooner.

Aaron was waiting for him in his throne room, looking much too relaxed. Shouldn't Aaron be afraid? Warrior Monks surrounded his Palace.

And although all of Thamon worshiped Aaron as a god, at the moment he was only a prisoner. Yes, the Palace was a nice jail. It was filled with gold and gems, and Aaron had enough food to last a lifetime thanks to the Blessed Ones. But still, he was a prisoner.

Before Sawdi had gone to his cabin, he had threatened Aaron, even thrown him around. So why wasn't he afraid?

"I am going after Stryker," Sawdi announced once they were both seated.

The announcement didn't surprise Aaron. It was what he was hoping Sawdi would do. Go away, take the Warrior Monks. Leave him in peace. Maybe Sawdi and Stryker would kill each other, and that would mean he would be the only ruler of Thamon. The thought of all that happening made him smile, and it pleased him to see Sawdi glance at him in surprise.

"Whatever you think is best," Aaron said, bowing to Sawdi. "While you are gone, is there anything you want me to do?"

The two men stared at each other. Both were trying to figure out what the other was thinking. Neither one of them believed that they were still friends.

Both knew that, in truth, they had never been friends. They had been collaborators. They both wanted power. They were both greedy. While it had served them to work together, they acted as if they were friends. But that time was over.

Aaron had finally discovered that Sawdi had been controlling him all along. And Sawdi knew he had always looked down on both Stryker and Aaron. He had been the wise one. He had directed the takeover of Thamon. He had made Aaron the god of Aaron-Lem.

Now Sawdi wondered if that had been his or the ring's decision. Perhaps he had never been in charge. Sawdi could barely think his hand hurt so much, and for a moment, the ring withdrew and gave him some relief.

But Sawdi knew the ring had only done that so he could continue to function as if he was in charge. The ring wanted him to make sure that Aaron stayed afraid, and not the smiling sycophant he was at the moment.

Neither Aaron nor Sawdi said anything. Both of them waiting for the other to make a move.

Now that the warm season had arrived, both Etar and Trin were higher in the sky, which allowed more light to pass through the windows, sending patterns of color onto the gold floor.

But the Warrior Monks blocked the lower half of the windows, so the display was much more subdued than the last time they had sat together in the throne room.

The silent lights danced on the floor as they both waited. Someone had to speak.

The Warrior Monk standing in the corner stirred slightly, and the ring shot a band of pain up Sawdi's arm, and he flinched. The pain receded, and Sawdi turned to Aaron and said, "But I am leaving the Warrior Monks here with you."

It pleased Sawdi to see the flash of fear in Aaron. Of course, Aaron had been hoping that the Monks would leave with him. That would release him from this prison.

Sawdi also realized that he, too, was pleased. He didn't want to travel with the Warrior Monks. Yes, they could sweep through the countryside killing, or whatever they did with the people since he had never seen remains.

Sawdi suspected that somehow the animals and people were absorbed into the Warrior Monks. Maybe what they killed was food for them.

If so, they must be starving since they hadn't moved since he had them surround the Palace. But then, perhaps that explained the lack of animal and bird life around the Palace. Or on the other hand, maybe it was because the Palace was a horrible place.

Suddenly, Sawdi realized how much he wanted to leave. Not later. Now. It was time. He would go after Stryker. He would find him and take the pendant.

At that thought, the ring sent a wave of cooling relief through his body. It had never done that before. Yes, this is what the ring wanted. It wanted to be reunited with the pendant.

It was a strange thought, but Sawdi knew that it was true. Why it was true, he didn't know. But if the ring would give him relief because of that decision, he would do it.

For himself, he would enjoy getting rid of Stryker and then come back for Aaron.

Sawdi couldn't admit to himself that it was possible that coming back for Aaron was not what the ring wanted. But he hoped that once he put the two items together, things would be better.

Perhaps wearing the pendant and the ring would give him all the power he had ever wanted. He could rule from his cabin with no one knowing it was him.

He could manipulate the hearts and minds of the people across all of Thamon without leaving home. The silent ruler. That's what he wanted. He hoped that was what the ring, and perhaps the pendant, had in mind for him.

"No," Sawdi said, finally answering Aaron's question, "I don't want you to do anything. At all. I'll be back, and we'll talk then."

Aaron stood as Sawdi walked out of the room. He didn't look back. If he had, he would have seen Aaron collapse back down into his throne. The Warrior Monk in the corner shivered, and Aaron knew that if that thing could feel, it shivered with happiness.

Aaron shivered too. But not from happiness. His ruse with Sawdi hadn't worked.

Baywolf walked into the throne room and saw Aaron slumped with worry. He knew that Aaron would feel more than worry if he knew who had arrived on Thamon.

Aaron looked up as Baywolf bowed and said, "My lord, what would you have me do?"

For the first time since he was at school with Sawdi and Stryker, Aaron didn't know what to say. At the moment, he had no idea what he needed Baywolf to do, so he said nothing.

Baywolf sat down in the chair that Sawdi had just vacated. Both of them were waiting to decide what to do next. Both of them unaware of the other's plans.

FORTY ONE

S tryker returned to his room after speaking to the Preacher at the Temple, if you could call that dinky building a Temple.

Stryker had thought he had recognized the man, but as he talked with him, Stryker realized that he didn't. The Preacher must remind me of someone else, he thought.

He was glad he didn't know him. That he hadn't been the one to teach him, because he didn't think he had been trained very well. For one thing, although he was subservient enough, there was something about him that put Stryker's teeth on edge.

When he had complained about the smallness of the Temple, the Preacher had smiled and said there weren't many people in Yeal Thalor. But all of them were of one mind.

One mind? What did he mean by that, Stryker asked himself. Must mean everyone had been converted to Aaron-Lem because he had seen the people bow to Aaron at the sound of the bell. Yes, Stryker mused, I think I will keep that practice alive once I am ruler.

Still, Stryker couldn't let go of his dislike for that Preacher and decided that once everything was in place, he would come back and eliminate him.

Stryker's mind was still on the Preacher when he glanced over at the table where he had left the open map and noticed that there was something on it.

Zonk, how did I miss that? How long had it been there? Stryker thought. He had lost time.

But then Stryker calmed himself down. He was the only one with a map. No one knew where he was. No one could stop him. It was only his excitement about getting closer to having the whole pendant that was making him anxious.

He had time. It was night. He could rest and start in the morning. Besides, he needed supplies. And he required guides. He had no idea what Turva was like having never been before. And if he was reading the map correctly, it was telling him to go up the mountain.

He had seen the mountain. It was massive. It loomed over the town. It looked close, but Stryker knew that it was probably much further away than it looked. And there must be a path that the locals would know about that would save him time.

Yes, he needed a guide or two. He'd go into town and ask for referrals. It didn't matter if they saw him find the pendant. They wouldn't have any idea what it was about or what would happen when he found it. Besides, he would be all-powerful by then. He could do whatever he wanted with anyone.

The next morning Stryker woke feeling almost as excited as he did that day when he was seven and followed the arrows that led him to the map. Stryker gathered the few belongings that he had and headed out into that stupid little town. He had seen men gathering in the tiny cafe. He'd go there.

For once, Stryker was pleased that no one knew who he was. They didn't know he had been the orchestrator of all the violence that happened on Thamon to convert everyone to Aaron-Lem. If they did, he might be in trouble. He had no backup.

The Preacher said he was without a Kai-Via since this was such a small town. And Stryker's only real skill was in manipulating how people thought so that they did his bidding.

But that was all Stryker needed right now. It would get him guides, and then it wouldn't be long before he had what he had come to Turva for.

After that, no one would be able to stop him.
****

The Preacher watched Stryker leave the boarding house and head to the cafe. Ian knew that Stryker wasn't so stupid as to start out without supplies and a guide.

Last night's reunion with his family was still filling Ian with happiness. But their job on Turva had just begun, and he couldn't let his joy at seeing his family after all these years take away his focus.

If they succeeded in this, they would have the rest of their lifetimes to celebrate. If they didn't, there would be no other lifetimes. That was what the prophecies had said, and he believed them.

He and his brothers had believed them when he sent the rest of their families away to the Sanctuary, and then let the rest of the world think that they had all died. Except for Udore. He wanted to be captured and taken to the center of Aaron-Lem. Udore's job was to gather the resistance in Edes and wait for the arrival of two women from another planet.

Now that Ian had met Meg and Suzanne, he knew the time was coming when the world would either explode or heal. How either one of those two scenarios happened, Ian didn't know.

He supposed that would have been too easy if they had all the information. All they would have had to do was follow the prophecies. But what fun would the two bored brothers have had with that?

Yes, he and Suzanne discussed the bored brothers, and he knew the story that she had told him was true. The brothers were the source of writings and the pendant and the ring. No, they weren't gods. Far from it. But they were from an advanced civilization, so they had the tools to do what they had done, delighting in their experiments and checking the results.

Suzanne had told Ian about what had happened on Erda. The brothers had been taken away, or gone away, after that. They would not be back to help or hinder in this situation.

Ian doubted that they had ever returned to Thamon to check what they had done. They probably never had time considering how many planets they had played with.

No, they were on their own for better or worse. Ian was sure it was for the better. He had men in place at the cafe, ready to volunteer to guide Stryker. Ian told the truth when he had told Stryker that the entire town of Yeal Thalor was of one mind.

But not the mind of Aaron-Lem. They were united as one in overthrowing the reign of Aaron-Lem, and returning the freedom of choice and thought to the people.

Joseph and Fionn were waiting for Ian in the back room. They had asked to return to the village with him. Udore thought that Ian could use more protection, and his daughter and nephew had agreed.

He had said yes to the security, as long as his daughter Rose came back with him. There was no point in all of them trudging up the mountain.

Besides, Rose would be of help once Sawdi arrived. Sawdi would never recognize her, having never visited the women of the Blessed Ones. But Rose knew of Sawdi, and she wanted to be part of the plan for stopping him.

How they would do that, none of them knew. Yet. Stopping Stryker would be easy compared to Sawdi. Ian bowed his head to his God, Ophey, the God of light, and asked for the wisdom to know what to do, and the courage to do it.

Forty Two

The seven of them had been walking for hours, and they had yet to reach the base of the mountain. They could see it looming above them. Meg couldn't see how they would ever get up it. It looked more like a series of cliffs with some straggly trees on it than the kind of mountains that were on Erda where she and Suzanne had lived.

But Wren had flown ahead and said that there were a series of switchbacks that they could take. Meg envied Wren's ability to fly ahead of them, or even to be able to fly back to town and check on Stryker's movements. When she thought about it, she realized that perhaps she was the only one who had to walk.

Suzanne could shift to being a dragon and easily make it up the mountain, and Udore and Tarek, as wizards, could go anywhere they wanted with the blink of an eye. Silke could fly ahead or ride on shoulders. Meg was the only one stuck walking. So why didn't the rest go ahead of her?

She was useless. Again.

A few seconds later, Karn came up beside her, huffing slightly now that the path had begun to rise.

"Not just you," Karn said.

"What?" Meg asked, turning to look at the man walking beside her. Everyone else was spread out on the path, walking at their own speed. Almost everyone was ahead of them.

"I have to walk too, Meg," Karn said.

"Oh," Meg said. "I forgot. But you gave up your powers on purpose and for such a good reason, to help the resistance. I didn't. I didn't choose to give up my abilities. They disappeared on their own."

Karn stopped, and Meg walked a few steps ahead of him before realizing what had happened. She turned around and said, "What?"

"You know what, Meg. You're being a brat again. Every once in a while, I see that ridiculous bratty child you must have been, and I feel quite sorry for Suzanne."

"Well," Meg spat back. "You should talk. I heard how you abandoned Wren. She thought you were quite selfish, too."

Karn stepped forward and grabbed Meg's hand, stood calmly looking at her, and then said, "Are you done now?"

Meg nodded. "I'm sorry. It's just that sometimes I feel so stupid and useless. Who I was is gone, and I keep hearing about the prophecies and my part in it, but no one will tell me what it is. So I either get mad, and then afraid because I might sprout fire again, or discouraged and irritated."

Karn put his arm around Meg, and the two of them started back up the path together.

"Will I know what my purpose is, Karn?" Meg asked, after they walked a little way together.

"Absolutely. I know you will. In fact, you are doing it now."

At Meg's incredulous look, Karn added, "I know it doesn't feel like it. But you are. You don't really believe that you and Suzanne are here by accident, do you?"

Meg sighed and shook her head. "I don't because none of you do. But even though I feel as if I didn't choose to lose my shapeshifter abilities, if I had to choose now, I would let them go to have all of you as friends."

Karn saw her looking up the path to where Udore and Tarek were walking together, father and son looking so much alike, their lean bodies moving in harmony together, with Silke flitting back and forth between the two of them.

"Karn," Meg asked, "Did Silke know that Udore was still alive? And if she did, why didn't she go to him? Isn't she bound to him for his lifetime?"

"You should ask her, Meg. But she and Udore decided that she would go with Tarek before Udore was captured, so she might not have known. On the other hand, perhaps she did, but she couldn't have stayed in prison with Udore."

"But if she did know, how did she keep that secret from Tarek? And now that they are both here, will she go back to Udore?"

"No," Karn answered, smiling at Meg. "She'll stay with Tarek. She had already transferred to Tarek. She might have chosen to not bind herself to another wizard after him, but now that you are in the picture, she will stay and wait for your children."

Meg didn't have time to ask Karn what he was talking about because there was a rustling in the trees, and Falcon swooped down and landed on Karn's shoulder.

Karn shouted at the others to stop, and then he had a silent conversation—to Meg—with Falcon. Meg could only guess at what Falcon was telling by watching Karn's face. It seemed to her that the ability to hear what a bird was saying was not only a beautiful gift but was very useful.

"First," Karn said, "Falcon says that he is not a bird, he is a man turned into a Falcon."

"Oh, sorry," Meg whispered back.

By then, the rest of the group had gathered around. Meg watched everyone's face and realized she was the only one not hearing what Falcon was saying.

Udore glanced over at Meg, who was looking very left out, and said, "You can hear him too. Would you like to?"

Meg nodded, and a second later, she heard him speaking. "Thank you," Meg whispered.

Falcon was reporting on both the Palace and Stryker. Meg realized that she had missed a large part of what he had said, but she did hear that Stryker had hired guides and would be coming up the mountain too. But the long way. The guides would make sure he struggled. They would have time to get to the pendant first.

After reporting, Falcon flew back down into the woods, saying he needed to rest before returning to the Palace. Traveling out of time was exhausting.

It was Tarek who turned to the group and said, "How can we avoid Sawdi?"

Seeing Meg's face, he added, "That's the part you missed. Sawdi is coming."

"With the Warrior Monks?" Meg gasped. "What are we going to do?"

Forty Three

"Getting past the Warrior Monks is going to be the hardest part," Bolong pushed into the minds of the three humans and four dragons that sat around him.

After dropping Sawdi off at the Palace, Bolong had come straight to the cave. Because of Baywolf's warning, he wasn't surprised to see people there, sleeping against the rock, including someone he knew.

Bolong couldn't believe how happy he was to see Dax. They had barely known each other at Stryker's training camp, but seeing each again under these new circumstances closed the distance between them.

Bolong and Dax were so delighted to see each other that they had done their best to hug. Not technically possible with a dragon, but they tried, dancing around the outside of the cave a bit before settling down.

Wren and Ruth watched them and tried not to laugh, but eventually, they gave up and broke down laughing. Their laughter triggered everyone else, including the dragons.

Dragon laughing is a cross between spitting steam and fire and trembling from head to toe, so Dax, Wren, and Ruth did their best to stay out of the way, dodging dragon tails and steam, which should have been frightening, but made them laugh all the harder.

Finally, the laughter died down, and the reality of the situation took over again. Bolong had told them that Sawdi was leaving for

Turva the next day. That would leave Ruth, Roar, and Dax free to get to Aaron.

"Did he tell you that he was taking all of you?" Ruth asked.

"No," Bolong replied. "But he usually does. He uses us to destroy everything. He likes doing it, it's not always necessary, but he does it anyway. For fun, I suppose.

"Of course, Sawdi doesn't know that we avoid hurting people. We produce lots of fire and smoke, but we miss hitting the people. On the other hand, this time, if the person he wants us to eliminate is Stryker, we will obey him. But after that, we will turn on Sawdi."

Bolong looked back at his friends, and they all nodded their massive heads in agreement.

"But, won't that keep you in dragon form for the rest of your lives?" Ruth asked.

"Probably. However, we have decided that it will be worth it if it means we can save Thamon from that ring."

"Ring?" Dax asked. "What ring?"

Bolong explained that they believed that it was the ring that Sawdi wore that was controlling him. Of course, he was already doing bad things before the ring, but Sawdi no longer seemed in control, and Bolong had seen the ring glow and send out streaks of light. He could also tell that Sawdi was in pain, and that had to be the ring.

"Who else knows about the ring?" Roar asked.

"Not sure if anyone does," Bolong answered.

"But you are sure it's where his power is coming from?" Dax asked. "You are willing to bet your life on it?"

"We are," answered Bolong, and the four dragons behind him snorted steam once again in agreement.

"Alright," Ruth said. "You are all willing to deal with Sawdi and stop him. We need to stop Aaron. Again, do you have any ideas on how we can get past the Warrior Monks?"

"I heard that one of you arrived as a dragon?" Bolong asked.

Roar nodded and said, "I did. But Ruth and I can be anything, so we could slip into the Palace as something that the Monks don't see. But what about Dax?"

Ruth said, "I can change his features for a bit if that would help.

"What if after Sawdi leaves with all of you, I make Roar look like you, Bolong, and make Dax look like Sawdi. Would it fool the Warrior Monks? Would they think that Sawdi had returned?"

Bolong thought for a while. "When they see Sawdi, the Monks start howling. Is it that they are seeing him, or feeling the ring? If it's the ring, it won't work, unless you find a way to make them believe that the man on the dragon is wearing that ring."

Dax felt hope well up inside of him. He could do it.

"If what they are feeling is a powerful projection of evil, I can do that. Inside of me, that evil is so strong sometimes it feels as if it is going to eat me up. I think I can send that out into the Warrior Monks for the few seconds that it takes to get past them," Dax said.

"But if they figure it out, won't they come after us even while we are in the Palace?"

For a moment, everyone was silent. It was Bolong who spoke. "I don't think so. I believe that Sawdi or the ring has forbidden them to go inside. Although Sawdi has one of the Monks guarding Aaron, Sawdi has never sent more of them into the Palace, even when Aaron made him mad.

I think that the Monk is not there to hurt him, only to scare him. I heard a rumor that Aaron tried to kill the Monk, and although it didn't work, the Monk didn't attack him back. Besides, once you get inside, you will have the help of Baywolf."

"Baywolf?" Dax asked. "Is that Bay? I thought he died at the training camp!"

"Aaron rescued him, and brought him to the Palace, and has been training him, keeping him a secret from everyone, including Sawdi. Aaron wanted Bay—yes, now Baywolf—to take over for

Stryker if something went wrong. Or if not Stryker, he would take over for you, Dax."

Roar looked at Ruth before asking, "Okay. Let me get this straight. This Baywolf is someone from Stryker's training camp. Someone you both knew. But Aaron has been secretly training him all this time. So Bolong, how do you know about him, and what makes you think he will help? Isn't he on the opposite side?"

Bolong looked at Dax and said, "Weren't you on the opposite side, Dax? And yet, here you are on our side.

"Karn found Baywolf when Karn was here pretending to be a blind Blessed One. When Baywolf learned all that Aaron and Aaron-Lem were doing, he became part of the resistance. Baywolf, Udore, Karn, and Rose had many meetings together."

At those words, all the blood drained out of Dax's face, and Roar had to catch him as he tilted towards the floor. After a few moments, Dax said, "Udore and Rose are here?"

"And who are Udore and Rose?" Roar asked.

"Maybe you better sit, Dax," Bolong responded. "I'm sorry for blurting that out. I had forgotten that you would not have heard since you came straight from the Islands. No, they aren't here. But they were. Sit. I'll tell you the story. Then we'll plan how to get you all into the Palace."

Forty Four

This is killing me, Stryker thought as he struggled up the mountain. Not that he had expected it to be easy. After all, finding the pendant had never been easy, but this was ridiculous. He was already exhausted, and they had only just begun.

Although the two guides that he hired were carrying all the supplies on their backs, he was the one that was huffing and puffing. He had to stop and rest with his hands on his knees so often he felt as if they had barely moved up the mountain.

In a way, they hadn't. The mountain loomed above him. So far to go. More than once, he had asked the guides if there wasn't an easier way. At first, he had asked politely, and they had assured him that there wasn't. That this way was the only way.

Now that they had been traveling for a day, he no longer asked politely. He screamed and yelled, but it changed nothing. They still assured him that this was the easiest way to get where he wanted to go.

Not for the first time, Stryker wished that he had magical abilities. It infuriated him that he didn't. Why not? The Mages and wizards he had killed because they did weren't any better than him. In fact, he was their superior in every way. Except that one.

But once he had all the pieces of the pendant, all that would change. Not only would he have magic, but he would also be magic. He would have all the power he ever desired. No more walking up zonking mountains. No more bowing to puffed-up ego-driven Aaron and that freak Sawdi Frey. Even the Warrior Monks would bow to him. Everyone would.

The pendant, swinging on a chain around his neck, seemed to agree with him. Sometimes it was so warm it hurt to have it directly on his skin, and he would have to put a piece of cloth around it. The part sewn into his cloak sometimes turned warm, too. Stryker wished that he could figure out why. Was it warning him? Wanting something?

Sometimes all of this hocus-pocus mystery stuff made him crazy. Like the map. Sometimes it showed him things, other times, it was blank, and all he could do was continue hoping that he was going in the right direction.

It was pointless not to allow the guides to see the map. It was why they were there, after all. They needed to know where the map was pointing them to, and then find the best route to get there.

They had questioned him about what he was looking for, and why the map didn't always work. He had told them in no uncertain terms that it was none of their business. They were there to get him to where he was going. After that, they were free to go. That's what he told them. But of course, that wasn't true. He would have to destroy them, like anyone else who got in his way.

However, although the map never showed a path, it did continue to point to one specific place, so that's where they were heading. The guides told Stryker that it was on the edge of a cliff. Near the top of the mountain, there was a massive canyon.

"How big a canyon?" Stryker asked.

One of the guides had pointed to Yeal Thalor and said, "Ten towns would fit into it stacked on top of each other and a hundred more side by side."

"And this map is pointing to that canyon?" Stryker asked, paling at the thought that he had to go up the mountain and then down into that canyon to get the pendant.

"We won't know until we get there," the guide had said. "But there are small caves and openings near the top, and perhaps this is where what we are looking for might be."

"There is no 'we'," Stryker snapped. "Only me."

The guide lifted both hands and backed away while Stryker glowered at him. Now that he knew that what he was looking for was in some massive hole in the mountain, Stryker knew he had to keep the guides happy. He would send them down to get it if he needed to.

Not for the first time, Stryker wondered who or what had hidden the pendant, and why? He figured that once he found it, he would have all the answers. But they probably wouldn't matter anymore, anyway.

What Stryker was barely admitting to himself was that he was terrified. He knew that Sawdi figured out that he hadn't died on the Island. Sooner or later, Sawdi would come for him. It wouldn't matter if it happened after he found the pendant piece, but if he came before then, he had no way of fighting him. No one would come to his rescue.

He had betrayed everyone and left them to die on the Islands. For a brief moment, Stryker thought about Dax and Ibris with sadness. He had loved them. He had considered them as his sons.

Yes, he was sorry about them, but the rest of the people left on the Islands were worthless. He hoped that after the Warrior Monks had finished killing off all the people, they had left the Islands as beautiful as when he had first been there.

He had decided that after he got the pendant, he would return to the Islands, and make them his home.

The two guides watched Stryker sitting against a tree gloating. They knew he thought that no one but him was going after the pendant, and soon he would have everything he needed.

They smiled at each other, their backs turned to Stryker, and one whispered to the other. "This is the perfect example of what you don't know will hurt you."

If it had been safe to do so, they would have laughed out loud. If they had been given permission, they would throw Stryker off the mountain and be done with it.

But Ian had told them that Stryker had to get to the pendant. He had even told them what day to be there. If they were going to make it, they would need to get Stryker moving, and perhaps it was time to take the shorter way. The sooner they got him there, the sooner all this would be over.

FORTY FIVE

Bolong said goodbye to Dax and the two shapeshifters. He hoped that he would see them again, but he doubted it.

He thought that even if they all succeeded in the long run, many of them would die before it was over. And he was willing for it to be him if it meant that people of Thamon would be free again.

Yes, he would like to have had a life with Suzanne on Thamon, but if he helped make it a good place for her to live, he would die happy.

He and his four friends circled the cave one time before heading to the Palace, dipping their wings in farewell. Dax, Ruth, and Roar, stood at the entrance to the cave waving at them. They would wait until they saw Bolong leave with Sawdi before going to the Palace, pretending to be them.

Sawdi was waiting for him on the roof of the Palace. Bolong didn't see Baywolf anywhere, but he knew that Baywolf would be watching and listening. While Sawdi was distracted, Bolong sent Baywolf a mind message about what they were planning, so that Baywolf would be ready to help Dax and his friends once they arrived.

Once in the air, Bolong circled the cave, much to Sawdi's displeasure. Seconds later, Sawdi sent them through time towards Turva.

It didn't take long before Bolong could see Turva in the distance, with its shoreline and the massive mountain ridge that rose in front of them.

Sawdi never told Bolong where they were going, but Bolong assumed that they were going to find Stryker. He hoped it wouldn't be anywhere near where Suzanne and that team were, but he and his friends had prepared a few scenarios of what they would do if that happened. But Bolong doubted that it would because as far as Sawdi knew, they had all died on the Islands.

Sawdi also knew that Stryker had escaped, and he had let him go. It occurred to Bolong that it wasn't Sawdi that let Stryker go, but the ring. Perhaps the ring wanted Stryker to find the pendant. In some strange way, that would make sense.

So as they neared Turva, Bolong expected Sawdi to start searching for Stryker. Instead, Sawdi seemed to know exactly where they were going. Bolong could feel Sawdi's glee. A few minutes later, it wasn't Stryker that they saw below them. Hidden in a cleft in the mountain, ringed by trees, was a group of people standing around a fire.

"No," Bolong screamed to himself. He knew where they were. It was the Sanctuary. Sawdi was going to destroy the Sanctuary. How did they miss this? How did they not know that Sawdi knew about the Sanctuary and where it was? Now, it was too late. If Sawdi had his way, he and his friends would have to kill everyone below them.

Praying that it would work, Bolong sent out waves of energy that only a Mage might feel. Suzanne had told him that many of the Mages who had been on the Islands had left with Gelon Morgan to come to the Sanctuary, where so many families had taken refuge.

Bolong knew that the people didn't see them yet, but perhaps they could feel him. He only had to reach one person. Bolong pushed harder as Sawdi slapped his heels into his side, urging him on.

****

Gelon was inside one of the little caves when he felt it, and knew that the time had come that they hoped would never happen. Sawdi had discovered the Sanctuary.

He and the Mages had fallen in love with the Sanctuary the moment they had arrived. It was set halfway up a mountain, on a plateau covered with trees, but with enough open space to plant crops. Small caves that went deep into the mountain circled the plateau. They used the caves for living and the storing of food.

When Gelon and his band of refugees first arrived, they were kept away for days by the guards that surrounded the Sanctuary. The leaders of the Sanctuary took their time evaluating them before allowing their entry.

The refugees had been upset. They were tired and hungry and recovering not only from their journey, but from their imprisonment on Hetale. But one day, the person who they assumed was the leader came out to where they were camped, shook Gelon's hand, and welcomed them. He apologized for the delay. But they couldn't be too careful. They had survived for years by being this thorough.

Gelon assured the man they called Jori that they all understood.

Once they were within the Sanctuary, they were helped in every way possible. The children were welcomed into the small school they had, and everyone donated clothing and food until the refugees were able to fend for themselves.

As the months passed, most of the refugees felt as if they would be happy to stay in the Sanctuary forever. It was so beautiful and peaceful it was easy to forget that Aaron-Lem ruled Thamon with an unforgiving iron hand.

When the crew members of the two ships arrived with supplies, they too were kept out of the Sanctuary until it was confirmed who they were. It didn't take long. They knew Leon. The reunion between the crew members and Leon and his men had been loud and prolonged.

And the crew members had brought news of the people who were now on Turva. The ones who had rescued the Mages had arrived to stop Stryker, which meant that Stryker was also on Turva. So they had increased their surveillance. The Mages took turns standing guard searching the skies, listening and watching for signs of trouble.

Which is why even though there was nothing to be seen, Gelon was already on high alert, and immediately felt Bolong's wave of energy. He recognized it as a warning sign, one that Suzanne had told them about before they left. She had told them it was the kind of sign she would send out to let them know she was coming.

But Gelon knew this wasn't Suzanne. However, it was a dragon, and it was a warning. Trouble was coming.

Scrambling out of the cave, he sounded the alarm. Other wizards had come running too. They had trained for this moment for so long everyone knew what to do.

They had not panicked, but they were afraid. Would the plan work? How many dragons were coming? Were they friendly?

It was the head of the Sanctuary who breathed out what they all were afraid to hear, "It's Sawdi, he has found us." In the distance, five dragons spitting fire roared into view, heading straight for them.

"It's time," Jori said.

Along with the other Mages, Gelon raised his hands to shield the Sanctuary. He thought about how he had told Wren that he was willing to die to save his people. He was. He just hoped he didn't have to.

Seconds later, fire and steam engulfed the camp, and the people were gone.

FORTY SIX

Ian stood with his arm around Rose, watching the sky to the east.

"It's begun," Ian said.

Rose nodded. What could she say? They were in Yeal Thalor and could do nothing to help the people in the Sanctuary. Either all the plans were in place, or they weren't.

But the massive flames that now shot out from the mountain confirmed that Sawdi and his dragons had arrived, and had done what Ian and his brother Jori had thought they would.

"You didn't tell Tarek that Dax's father is still alive. Why not?"

Ian turned to his daughter. It had been so long since he had seen her. The things that Rose had endured at Aaron's hands, he couldn't begin to make right. But she, like many of the others, had made a choice. He had wanted Rose to go with his brother, Jori, and the rest of the family to the Sanctuary. But Rose had refused.

She didn't want to hide. She wanted to fight. Although they didn't know the extent of the horror that Aaron, Stryker, and Sawdi would unleash on the Islands, they knew that they had to stop them.

The prophecies had told them of the signs. It had warned them that each person would have to choose which side they would be on. Rose, along with Ian, Udore, and Jori, had decided to stand against Aaron-Lem. And they had chosen not to tell Tarek, Dax, and Ibris that they were still alive.

It was the hardest decision they had made. But it felt to them as if it was the best way to keep the rest of their families safe. It made sense that Jori would lead the families to the Sanctuary and keep them safe there. His gift was keeping people calm and providing for them. Perhaps those were not magical skills, but they were just as important. Essential for survival.

Ian and Udore had kept track of what happened to their sons, but Jori didn't know. He and the rest of the members of the family at the Sanctuary were cut off completely. On purpose.

That meant that Jori did not know that his son, Dax, had become one of the prime enforcers of Aaron-Lem. Jori had no idea that an intense need for violence drove Dax.

Ian knew that if the Mages had told him about Dax after they arrived, it had broken Jori's heart. He hoped it hadn't broken his spirit.

Once Ian became one of Aaron-Lem's preachers after talking his way into one of Stryker's training camps, he learned more about where the boys had gone.

To get into the camp, he had made himself look much younger, so that he appeared to be the same age as the other boys that Stryker was training. Stryker rarely visited the training camp he had chosen, so he hadn't worried about being recognized by him.

Yes, it had been difficult hiding his age, and the fact that he was a wizard, but the plan had worked. It had taken time, but eventually, he had gotten himself assigned to the Temple near the Sanctuary.

The plan had worked so far. Now they were here, almost all together again. That is if the Sanctuary had survived.

"I didn't tell Tarek, because he has too much on his mind already," Ian answered.

Both he and Rose knew that Tarek and the people traveling with him would have seen the fire, and guessed what it was.

"Don't lose hope," he whispered to Tarek.

He knew that Tarek couldn't hear him, but it was the best that he could do. He was also saying it to himself. So much of the plan they had designed so many years ago held the possibility of failure.

Looking up at the fire again, that now seemed to engulf the entire section of the mountain, Ian prayed that this part of the plan had worked.

Sawdi would now look for Stryker. In doing so, he would also find the group of people who needed to get the pendant before he discovered them.

"Keep going, Tarek," Ian whispered again, tightening his arm around Rose.

****

It was Karn who said, "We have to keep going."

They had heard the boom of the pine trees exploding as they burst into flames. They couldn't see over the mountain to see what was burning, but Udore knew, and when Tarek saw his face, he figured it out and fell to his knees.

"What's happening?" Meg screamed.

"It's the Sanctuary, isn't it?" Suzanne asked.

Udore nodded, and Karn repeated, "We have to keep moving. We still have to get to the pendant before Stryker. And now that Sawdi is here, he will be looking for Stryker, and in the process, he will find us."

Karn had already started to move up the trail when Tarek yelled after him to stop. "But what about all the families, and Leon and his men, and the crew of Eos. What of them?"

It was Udore who answered him, Karn still moving away. "There was a plan in place, Tarek. If they followed it, they are safe. If it didn't work, we still have to do our part. All those families and our friends are counting on us.

"Besides, you know that Stryker saw those flames. He will know that means Sawdi is here, and he'll be moving faster, too. Come on, son. We have to go."

Meg reached out her hand. Tarek took it, and the three of them followed Karn up the mountain. All of them knew that there was no time to waste, but Tarek struggled with guilt and despair, hoping against hope that the massive plan that Karn, his father, and his uncle had put into place would work. Otherwise, they were all lost.

FORTY SEVEN

T he seven of them hurried up the mountain, spurred on by Karn. Although they couldn't see the fire, the smoke filled the air, making it harder to breathe. Finally, Karn, seeing everyone struggling, stopped and pointed to a small clearing a few feet from the path.

"We'll stop here for the night. The dragons will be tired from traveling and destroying, so Sawdi will have to let them rest. We might as well do the same."

Meg was delighted with the idea but asked anyway, "But what of Stryker?"

It was Wren who answered her, gliding down out of the sky as a raven, and shifting back to herself. At least the form that they all knew.

Karn smiled and rushed to her side, holding her hand as she answered.

"The guides are slowing him down. In some ways, he is slowing himself down. Even though he believes that putting the pieces of the pendant together will give him all the power he needs to stop Sawdi, there is still the fear that it might not work."

"Will it?" Meg asked. "If he puts the pendant together, will it give him all the power he needs to rule the world?"

Turning to Suzanne, Meg asked, "Would the bored-brothers have made something that powerful just to entertain themselves? And the ring? Were they, are they, that terrible?"

"At this point, I don't think the bored-brothers are around to be entertained. As far as I know, they are no longer roaming the galaxies causing trouble. But yes, they were that advanced and that terrible. At least one of them repented, but that doesn't help this situation.

"What they left on this planet could destroy it. Or at least that's my understanding. Is that what the prophecies say, Udore?"

By then, the group had moved to the clearing, each one of them having found a place to sit to rest.

"Yes," Udore answered. "Not that they mention bored-brothers in the silver snake-shaped spaceship, but I agree, now that you have told us about them, this is their handiwork."

"I have a question, Udore," Meg said. "I understand that there were people, your family especially, that knew of the prophecies, and because of that, you made choices. You made a plan. Then Karn joined in on your plan. But if you knew what Aaron-Lem was going to be about, why not put the plan into action years ago? Why wait so long to actively rebel?"

Silke flew to Udore's shoulder as if she was giving him the signal to answer.

Udore looked over at Tarek, smiled, and then to Meg sitting beside him.

"We were waiting for you," Udore said.

"That's ridiculous," Meg answered. "Why me?"

"Well, we didn't know it would be you. We only figured that part out for sure after you sent out that beam of light. It was seen all over Thamon, and that was the trigger."

"But I didn't do that," Meg protested. "It happened. I don't remember it. All I remember is being surrounded by fire, and Karn pushing me into the ring of Mages. Maybe they did it."

"They didn't. Karn pushed you into the center because he knew that they would help project it. Without thinking about it, that's what they did. When Karn learned that you and your sister came from another planet, he suspected that you were the ones we have been waiting for.

"We knew the Islands were where you would arrive, and since all the other signs, like the takeover of Aaron-Lem, pointed to this being the time, he went to the Islands to find you.

"That's why we were all there?" Tarek broke in, holding Meg's hand as she squeezed her eyes shut, hoping that some of it would make sense to her soon. She didn't feel like the reason for anything, let alone a prophecy. Her shapeshifting gifts were long gone, and although she sometimes felt the fire burning within her, she had no control over it or any beam of light. She was Ordinary now.

Udore smiled at Meg, who had looked up to hear the answer from him. Suzanne had moved to sit on the other side of Meg, and together they waited to hear what Udore had to say.

"Yes, that's why you were all there. Whether you consciously chose to be there or not, you were all on the Islands for a purpose. Including Dax and Ibris, and even Stryker."

"But why am I here?" Meg asked. "Was it just to be used as a beam to tell you all it's time to put the plan into action? Is that why I am not a shapeshifter anymore?"

This time it was Silke who answered Meg. Still sitting on Udore's shoulder, she said, "No. It's more than that.

"Yes, the light beam shielded the Islands. Sawdi thought everyone had died. And the beam also told everyone watching for it that you had arrived. But no, your job is not over.

"It's you, Meg, who has to destroy the pendant and the ring. At least that is what the prophecies have told us. 'A young woman from another planet will destroy the two symbols of evil, freeing Thamon from the hold of a false religion and the three men who conspired together to be all-powerful.' That's you."

"But how?" Meg wailed.

"That's where faith comes in, my dear," Udore said. "We don't know. All we know is that we have to get the ring and the pendant to, or near you, so you can destroy them."

Meg dropped her head and whispered to herself, "Oh my gods."

Suzanne put her arm around Meg and addressed Udore. "That's what this is all about? You want Stryker and Sawdi to be in the same place at the same time, and then you expect Meg to destroy the pendant and the ring, and probably kill them in the process? Are you zonking crazy?"

"Not crazy," Karn answered. "And yes, that is what we are trying to do. It will work. It has to."

The seven of them stared at Meg slumped against her sister, her eyes closed, trying not to cry, and hoped that they were doing the right thing.

No one hoped more than Meg did. There was no way this was going to work. They were all going to die, and it would be her fault.

FORTY EIGHT

"We were waiting for you, too, Suzanne," Karn said. "Or at least, we knew that there would be two of you. Your role wasn't—isn't—so clearly defined."

Udore added, "Perhaps it was to let us know about the story of the bored brothers. We had always wondered who had written the prophecies. Even if the brothers were not the authors, someone else could have written it."

Meg's head had snapped up at the mention that Suzanne was part of the prophecies. "Even if what you say is true, how would anyone have possibly known all this was going to happen? It doesn't make any sense. No one can make a whole planet follow a story that they wrote out. And no one has a crystal ball into the future."

Everyone was silent, thinking about what Meg had said when Tarek spoke up. "But what if this has happened before, and they wrote it down knowing it would happen again?"

"What?" Meg said. "Wouldn't I remember that? Or all of you remember doing this before. Do you? I know that I don't."

"Well, I don't," Wren said, speaking for the first time. "But it doesn't have to be a conscious memory, does it? I know things that I can't answer how I know.

"But then, I have lived a long time, so perhaps that is because I have had so much experience."

"That could be one answer," Silke said. "I, too, have many things that I know, yet I don't remember how I learned them. But I have also lived a long time, through many generations of wizards, so it seems likely that I have accumulated some stories and knowledge from all of that.'"

"Well, there is another possibility," Suzanne said, joining in on the conversation. "Perhaps it happened in another dimension on this planet. In Erda, we know how to travel between dimensions. The same kind of portal that brought me here to this world could have also transported me to another dimension."

"Like when you used to travel between the dimensions of Earth and Erda," Meg broke in.

"Yes, like that. That may be how the prophecies were written," Suzanne answered.

"Well then, why not tell us how to destroy the pendant and ring?" Meg asked. "It would make this so much easier."

"But then that wouldn't fulfill the brother's terms of the experiment, would it?" Karn said.

"Whether this happened before and is repeating itself here on Thamon, or whether it happened in another dimension, I don't want it ever to happen again anywhere," Meg said. "If I am required to destroy them to stop it forever, then I am willing to do what needs to be done."

"Well, what needs to be done right now is rest," Wren said. "Everyone will need all their strength and ability to think clearly tomorrow. Ian, Rose, Joseph, and Fionn are watching over Yeal Thalor tonight so that I can stay here. I'll take the first watch. I haven't been climbing mountains all day."

"I'll watch with you," Karn said, and Wren smiled at him in gratitude. Everyone pulled sleeping bags and some dried fruit out of their packs and settled down for the night. They still had the element of surprise on their side, so there could be no fire or anything else that might alert either Stryker or Sawdi to their presence.

****

Further down on the mountain, Stryker pulled his cloak tighter and tried not to feel sorry for himself. The guides had told him that they could not light a fire because the dragons might see them.

Then they had proceeded to ask Stryker so many questions he wanted to throw them off the mountain.

"How could there be dragons? Weren't dragons outlawed in Thamon? Weren't they all dead? Who were those dragons, and why would they set part of the mountain on fire?

"What was there that they destroyed? Why were they here? Would the dragons come after them?"

Stryker had told them he didn't know the answers to any of those questions, but agreed that it was safer not to light a fire. After that, he just glared at them until they shut up.

Now the three of them were huddled inside a hollow tree that they had found. It was better than being out in the open, but the two men were so close to him it made Stryker want to scream. The sooner he found the pendant, the better. Then he would never have to be around anyone inferior to him again.

He pulled the hood of his cloak up over his head and lowered his forehead to his knees. He needed to sleep. When Sawdi found him, and he did not doubt that he would, he needed every one of his senses awake and alert.

He didn't plan to fight Sawdi. He planned to outsmart him. But if he had to fight, he would. One thing Stryker was glad about: he didn't see or hear a single Warrior Monk. There would be no reasoning with the Monks. There might be with Sawdi. However, what would solve all his problems was getting to the pendant before Sawdi and his zonking dragons found him.

The two guides waited until Stryker had dropped his head to his knees before looking at each other. They both looked down at the sleeping man and winked at one another. Of course, they knew all the answers to all the questions they had asked.

Their goal had been to get under his skin, which had turned out to be marvelously easy. Now they just had to stay away from Sawdi and the dragons until the girl and the others reached the cliff. Ian had told them that the solution to destroying the pendant and Stryker would be there waiting for them.

Yes, they were leading Stryker to his death. Perhaps their own too, but it would be worth it if they could free Thamon.

Just before falling asleep, one of the men glanced up inside the hollow tree trunk and realized that he could see the stars shining through a hole in the tree.

He took it as a good sign when one star shot through the sky. He would take every good sign that he could get that all would be well. He sighed, leaned back, and forced himself to fall asleep.

FORTY NINE

"Are you ready?" Ruth asked Dax and Roar.

Dax nodded yes and then did something that surprised even him. He shook hands with both of them. Nothing needed to be said. No matter what their pasts had been, no matter what Dax had done to them and their friends and family, that was then. This was now. They needed to be a team without any divisions between them for their mission to work.

Ruth put her arms out and gathered both men into a hug. Dax almost cried. He couldn't remember the last time someone had hugged him. It was certainly not part of the daily curriculum at Stryker's training camp.

Ibris had tried a few times, but Dax had pushed him away. Afraid then, as he was now, that he would start crying and never stop.

Since the moment his parents died, his life had never been the same. What would his dad, Jori, say to him now if he were still alive? Dax wondered. He hoped that his father would forgive his past sins and think of him as someone who, in the end, tried to do the right thing.

Roar shifted into a dragon and Ruth into a tiny mouse. She would need to stay hidden on the journey to the Palace, and close enough that she could mask both Roar and Dax's identity until they were inside.

On the way, in their own way, all three of them prayed that the Warrior Monks would think they were Bolong and Sawdi. As they neared the Palace, they could hear the angry hum of the Monks.

If the Warrior Monks didn't believe the deception, the Monks would suck them down into the writhing mass of white beings and absorb them. It had to be painful. They had all heard what happened that night when the Monks sucked up the birds and animals who had not made it to a shelter on Lopel.

None of them would forget the terror of that night as they huddled together, hoping that the Mages would shield them. But there was no Mage or wizard or light beam to protect them now. It was just them.

The humming grew louder, and then the Warrior Monks began to shriek. The sound raised both terror in their hearts and hope. If they were shrieking because they thought it was Sawdi, it was a good thing.

Roar did what Bolong had told him to do. He dipped his wings, and the shrieking got louder. It was working. With only a few feet to go to the roof, the sound was so loud Roar thought he would faint and fall out of the sky, but he managed to land. Dax slid off him while Ruth scurried away to the edge of the roof where no one would see her, but she could watch the sky.

Dax walked across the roof, and when he was hidden from view, he turned to Roar and raised his hand to the dragon, who nodded his massive head in return. Roar could not come with them. Bolong would not have remained on the roof. He would have returned to the cave. They had to do exactly what the Warrior Monks would expect.

Ruth gathered every bit of reserve energy that she had and kept Roar looking like Bolong as he flew back to the cave. Once there, he would return to the Palace in another disguise.

If he could find a way in, he would. Otherwise, his orders were to stay safe. Ruth's job was to protect Dax as he went to stop Aaron.

But none of them knew what to do about the Warrior Monks. The only person who could control them was no longer on Edes.

However, they would cross that bridge when they came to it. Perhaps if the other team on Turva were successful and destroyed the ring, that would also destroy the Warrior Monks. Only time would tell.

Ruth sent one last blessing out to Roar and turned to Dax, who was standing at the top of the stairs that led down into the heart of the Palace. Facing him was another man Ruth had never seen before. Based on what they had heard about him, it had to be Baywolf.

The two men didn't turn to look at Ruth as she shifted back into herself. They were too busy sizing each other up. Ruth waited, and when it seemed as if they were going to stare at each other forever, she finally sighed and said, "Good gods, could you two get over yourselves? We have a job to do."

Ruth reached out a hand to Baywolf, who grasped her hand between his two hands that were as big as her face and bowed to her.

"Thank you for coming, Ruth. I have heard of you."

Ruth wanted to ask how, but then thought of all that Udore and Karn had known and decided that was probably a story for another time. If they survived this, they would have plenty of time to catch up with what they both knew.

"We know very little about you, Baywolf. Bolong only told us that you were trained by Aaron to be Stryker's or Dax's replacement. But despite that, you are on the side of the resistance? Before we face Aaron, could you tell us why? Bolong trusted you, but should we?"

Baywolf turned back to Dax and bowed. "Sorry, I was a little shocked to see the man that I was trained to replace. For years, I imagined you as some kind of god. But you are just a man like me."

Dax laughed despite himself, "A god. Not even close. Just a man who has lost his way and wants to make some of it right again."

"Then, in that, we are brothers, Dax," Baywolf said and turned to Ruth.

Ruth took one look and said, 'Okay. That's enough for now. Let's do this before someone discovers we are here. Bolong said that you could get us in front of Aaron through secret passages?"

At Baywolf's nod of agreement, Ruth turned to Dax and said, "Are you ready?"

"Yes." Dax said. He couldn't say one more word. Otherwise, he might lose his courage, and that was the one thing he was not willing to do.

FIFTY ONE

B aywolf led Dax and Ruth down a long flight of twisting steps, before coming to a stop in front of what looked like a solid stone wall. But Baywolf didn't pause. He walked right through it.

Ruth and Dax looked at each other in amazement. What had just happened? Then an arm stuck itself out of the wall and pulled them in. A second later, they were all standing in a small circular room, and Baywolf was laughing at them.

"Shocked you, didn't I? I've been waiting for years to be able to do that to someone," he said, his green eyes bright, even in the low light.

Dax turned around the room and then back to Baywolf before saying, "Maybe you better explain yourself before we go any further."

Baywolf gestured at a bench on one side of the room and waited until Dax and Ruth had taken a seat. He stayed standing, his massive arms crossed over his chest.

There was a small window set in line with the bench, and Dax and Ruth could see out to where the Palace was surrounded by Warrior Monks, a white mass breathing as one being.

Gesturing at the swirling Monks, Ruth asked, "Can't they see us in here?"

Baywolf leaned back against the stone wall and closed his eyes. He knew what Dax and Ruth were seeing. A large man with an ugly face, the face that had isolated him from the other boys at the training camp.

He had pretended not to hear them because it was easier to ignore the taunts. It hadn't been the same camp where he knew Karn, Dax, and Ibris had been trained. But he was sure that all of Stryker's camps were the same. Bullies learning to be better bullies. That some of them had learned how to survive amid that terror was a miracle. That some of them were now willing to rebel against what Aaron, Stryker, and Sawdi had done, was even more miraculous.

Baywolf counted his survival as a miracle. Aaron rescuing him from the camp was not what he had expected. He had expected to die the day he beat the other boy senseless. It was the day he had lost control of himself. It had never happened since then. Now, if he had to be violent, he chose it, not the other way around.

Through the years, he had let Aaron train him, but when Aaron wasn't looking, he taught himself. Although he could barely remember his childhood before the training camp, over time, he got glimpses of what it had been like.

And after remembering that it had included magic, Baywolf looked for that in himself, hoping against hope that he was something more powerful than what Aaron wanted him to be.

While Aaron trained him to be stealthy and secretive, and use violence when needed, Baywolf trained himself first to find and then use magic. The invisible door and window were the result of what he had learned how to do. Hide. And watch.

That's how he had discovered that Udore was a wizard, and was staying in jail by choice, while he, Rose, and Karn planned a rebellion.

Baywolf hadn't revealed himself to them because he wasn't sure at first what side he would be on. After all, Aaron had rescued him. Didn't he owe Aaron something? However, over the years, he had watched Aaron become increasingly power-hungry and lose the few magical abilities he once had because of his greed.

He didn't want to lose the magic he had found and practiced. Magic was his only tie to the memory of where he had come from. Still, he waited. The element of silence and surprise was something he treasured. Besides, he didn't know how anyone could take Thamon back.

It all changed the day that Bolong spoke to him. Bolong had seen Baywolf hiding on the roof and talked to him, not out loud, of course, in his head. That was an entirely new experience for him.

Since coming to the Palace, only Aaron had spoken to him, and he had never experienced mind-talk before with anyone. It had taken him a few moments to realize that the words had come from a dragon. It had never occurred to him that Bolong was more than what he appeared to be. That all the dragons in Sawdi's crown were also men.

They only exchanged a few words before Sawdi returned. But after that, Baywolf made sure he was on the roof when Bolong arrived. Because they never spoke out loud, no one heard them, and if anyone were watching, they would have never known that a conversation was going on.

But there was. And over time, Bolong became his one and only friend. His first friend. Someone he could trust. It was through Bolong that Baywolf learned of all the horrors that Aaron-Lem was doing in the world.

It was Bolong who told Baywolf that someday he would have to choose. Would he remain Aaron's, or would he fight for freedom?

When Bolong put it that way, there was no need to wait for a decision. He wanted freedom. Baywolf had dreams of being free. Maybe even finding his family. Perhaps they still lived.

Bolong had told him about the Sanctuary on Turva. If they weren't there, possibly they would be in one of the others scattered around Thamon. Places where people had gone to hide, waiting for enough people to fight the evil that had taken over Thamon.

Yes, it had been an easy decision once Bolong explained the situation. He wanted freedom. He would fight for freedom. For himself. For the people in the Sanctuaries. And that would mean defeating Aaron.

Baywolf opened his eyes and looked at Dax and Wren, patiently waiting for him to tell them what they were doing, trusting him to do the right thing.

"Aaron knows you are here," Baywolf said. "Which means we have to do something he doesn't expect."

"What?" Ruth asked.

"Not show up. Aaron can't find us here. Besides, I need to hear your plan for stopping him and the Warrior Monks."

Dax looked at Ruth and cleared his throat. "I have a weapon to use against Aaron. The same one he uses. But we didn't know that the Warrior Monks would be here."

Baywolf laughed and said. "Good thing I have a solution for that problem."

FIFTY

Aaron didn't know whether to laugh or cry. Sitting in his throne room, he waited for the people who were coming for him. He wanted to laugh because he was so much smarter than them, and cry because he saw that Baywolf was one of them.

On the other hand, perhaps Baywolf was playing them, in which case he could forget the crying and start laughing. But he had to do it quickly because he wanted to look frightened when Dax arrived. Dax and some woman he had never seen before. No matter. They were no match for him.

So Aaron laughed as hard as he could. He hoped that the Warrior Monk who occupied the corner of the room would do something, anything. Twitch. Wiggle. Make a noise. But it never did. It just stared at him with the black holes that passed for eyes that followed him everywhere.

How Sawdi had raised people from the dead and turned them into these horrible things, he didn't know. Or even why. Well, he probably knew why. They were such efficient killing machines. No one could hurt them, and only Sawdi could control them.

Aaron laughed again. What if the Warrior Monk was going to protect him? Wouldn't that be a perfect scenario? That brooding white thing could help him destroy the people coming now to get him, because Aaron was sure that this wasn't a social visit.

Aaron had heard the shrieking of the Monks and thought that Sawdi had returned. He had a brief moment of hoping that Sawdi had come back to take the Monks with him, so he had opened the seeing tube he had built into one of the walls of this throne room to see what Sawdi was doing on the roof.

He had a few of these tubes built into the walls of the Palace. He built them before he encrusted the walls with the precious gems he had brought to him from all over Thamon.

If he were magic, he could have seen everywhere without the tubes, but he wasn't anymore. All the magical skills he once was so proud of had slowly drained away so that he had to resort to things like a seeing tube.

The tubes were not as good as magic, but they served a purpose. He could watch various parts of the Palace without leaving his throne room, or the bedroom where he had other tubes installed. The men who had installed them for him were long gone, turned to ash when their job was done and swept up by the Blessed Ones.

It was the tube to the roof that Aaron used the most because it was where he could see Sawdi arrive and try to gauge his mood. Not that it had ever helped. Sawdi was expressionless like his Warrior Monks.

At first, seeing the dragon, Aaron believed that it was Sawdi and Bolong. But a split second later, he realized that it was Dax and another dragon, not Bolong. Not that anyone but Sawdi rode Bolong.

Imagine that, Aaron thought. What will Sawdi say when he learns that there is another dragon on Thamon? Probably capture it for himself. It gave Aaron a thrill to think of Sawdi being surprised by something.

Although he hadn't expected a dragon, this turn of events did not surprise Aaron. He had anticipated that Dax might eventually come to get him. It was what he himself would do, after all.

But the dragon was surprising, and so was the woman. It would be interesting to see what Baywolf would choose to do. Would he surprise Aaron, too, or fulfill what he had trained him to do?

****

Across the ocean, Ibris felt as if a hand was squeezing his heart, making him feel faint. Beside him, Oiseon grabbed his shoulder to keep him from falling.

The two of them were sitting on Ibris' favorite bench on the beach, watching the waves lap gently against the white sand and Etar rise in the east. It had been peaceful, both of them content to listen to the water swoosh in and out over the pebbles embedded in the sand, the white foam fizzing and then dissipating.

They sat on the bench, not speaking. It was their quiet time of day before their work began. Ibris, as the Preacher, and Oiseon as the leader of the Mages, would try to keep the people calm while they waited to hear the latest about Aaron, Stryker, and Sawdi.

Falcon had come to tell them that everything was progressing as planned. But that had been days ago. Had Dax, Ruth, and Roar arrived on Edes?

Did the Eos make it to Turva? Would they find the pendant before Stryker?

The fact that Ibris didn't know that members of his family, that he had thought died long ago, were even now fighting for the resistance was a good thing. Otherwise, he might have actually fainted from the fear.

Because it was fear that had gripped his heart. Something was happening, and he had to help. Turning to Oiseon, he said, "Get the Mages. Get everyone willing to help the rebels and meet me at the market."

Oiseon didn't ask why. He knew.

The time had come, and now they needed to do their part.

FIFTY TWO

Meg and Tarek stood together, looking at the map. Udore had given it to Tarek after telling him that he was the one that had to go with Meg to get the pendant. The rest of them would be watching for Stryker and Sawdi, and hold them off as long as they could.

Udore had taken Meg aside and told her all that he knew about what the prophesies had said she would need to do. To Meg's question whether Udore was positive that she was the one that needed to do this thing, he answered without hesitation that yes, she was the one.

Although the writings didn't mention Meg or Tarek by name, all the signs pointed to Meg as the one who had to find the pendant and then destroy it, although the man with her could provide support and protection.

"I didn't know it was my son that would be doing this," Udore had said to her. "But even if I had, I couldn't have done anything to stop it. But now that I have met you, Meg, I am proud to know you, and it pleases me that you and Tarek have found each other again."

"Again?" Meg asked.

"Ah. Well, it depends on what you believe, child, but yes, I do think we find each other again as we move from lifetime to lifetime."

Udore waved his hand towards the group of people waiting for them, and said, "Like them. All of them. Together again. You and I, together again."

"But I don't remember any of this," Meg said. "However, I think I know what you mean about knowing people before. On Thamon, everyone has felt so familiar, even though we were strangers."

When Udore nodded at her, she added, "But then, I don't want to do this same thing over and over again. Can't we be done with it?"

"Yes. I believe you can finish it now, and then your next lifetimes will not include this kind of trouble. Now is the time, Meg," Udore said, handing her the map.

Meg thought about what Udore had said as she and Tarek studied the map. She knew that Udore, Wren, Karn, Silke, and Suzanne were watching them from somewhere in the woods.

They had hiked all day to reach this spot, and they were all exhausted. But there was no time to rest. Stryker was right behind them, and if Stryker was near, so was Sawdi.

The problem they were having was that the map was showing them that the pendant was directly beneath them, which didn't make any sense. They were standing on the ledge that looked out over a massive cavern.

Meg had accidentally kicked a stone over the edge and had listened to it fall as it bounced down the sides of the cliff. It took a long time to reach the bottom.

Looking out over the chasm, Meg could see what looked like tiny openings in the sides of the cliff.

"Could those be caves?" she asked, pointing to the closest one. "What if the last piece of the pendant is in a cave right below us?"

Meg dropped down to the ground, sharp stones cutting her hands and knees as she crawled to the edge and looked over. She wanted to be sick. Something she had never told anyone was that she was terrified of heights.

Yes, she had flown as a bird and even a dragon, but that was different than being a human, used to standing on the solid ground, seeing empty space below and having no wings. Grasping the edge of the cliff, she pulled herself across the ground, trying not to cry out as stones cut through her clothes.

Tarek had grabbed her feet, so she moved further out off the edge, shaking so hard she thought Tarek would not be able to hold on. Finally, she was far enough out that she could see a small cave directly below them. It had to be where the pendant was. But the opening was about ten feet straight down. How would she ever get there?

Once again, she mourned the loss of her shapeshifting abilities. If she could still turn into a bird, she could fly into the cave, find the pendant and bring it out so that everyone could help her destroy it. But she couldn't shapeshift anymore. She knew that Udore had told her that this had to be done by her, and her alone, but she had no idea how to get the pendant, and then how was she supposed to destroy it?

"One step at a time," she heard Udore tell her.

Tarek could support and protect her, just as he was holding her feet so she wouldn't fall over the edge, but he couldn't do it for her. She would have to find another way to get into the cave.

Wiggling backward, she edged away from the edge, and once it was far enough away, stood and walked into Tarek's arms, shaking with fear and determination.

"I think I know how I can get into the cave, Tarek," Meg said.

Taking off her torn cloak, she started ripping it into long strips of material. "Help me braid these pieces together and make a rope, and then you can lower me down."

"But then I can't go with you," Tarek said.

"No, you can't. I have to do this myself," Meg answered.

Tarek nodded, and the two of them worked together to make a rope. When they were done, Tarek tied one end of it around Meg's waist and the other end around a Stonenut tree that grew not far from the edge. If Meg slipped, he could pull her back up.

Tarek grabbed the coil of the rope, Meg stood facing him, and then backed off the cliff, trying to keep her feet on the side of it while leaning away. For a moment, she felt as if she would faint. She was parallel to the ground, her feet sliding on the sides of the cliff.

Tarek spoke gently in her mind, "I've got you, Meg. I won't let you go. Find the pendant, and I'll pull you back up."

Watching from the woods, Suzanne wanted to run out and help. Udore put his hand on hers and shook his head. "You need to help in another way," he whispered.

A few seconds later, Suzanne understood what he meant. In the far distance, she heard a sound only another dragon would recognize. Sawdi and Bolong were on their way.

"Be safe, Meg, but hurry up," she whispered to her sister, grateful that Meg couldn't hear what she could—the sound of dragons, and Bolong's warning that they were near.

Fifty Three

S tryker staggered into the clearing. He had practically run the rest of the way up the mountain, leaving the guards far behind him. He no longer needed them. When the map stopped being so cryptic and showed him the last part of the path to the pendant, he had forgotten about everything except getting to where he was going.

As he ran, his cloak caught on a tree branch, but he ignored it. The only important thing was the map clutched in his hand and the pendant pieces. One around his neck, the other transferred to a pocket in his pants.

He was so close he could almost taste it. Years of searching were coming to an end. The countless times that Aaron or Sawdi treated him as less than themselves were soon to be over. He, and he alone, would soon be the ruler of Thamon.

As he emerged from the woods, he glanced at the map and then turned in the direction of the cavern. But as he stumbled into the clearing, what he saw made him gasp and almost drop the map.

Someone was standing on the edge of the cliff. How could someone else be here?

No one but him knew about this place. Stryker calmed himself, folded the map, put it into his pocket, and started walking towards the man, telling himself that this was probably someone admiring the view. No one he needed to worry about.

The man was so busy holding onto a rope that he didn't notice Stryker. As he got closer to him, Stryker realized the man looked like the wizard Tarek. But that wasn't possible. Tarek had died on Lopel, along with everyone else.

Whatever the man was doing, he was standing right on top of where the pendant was supposed to be. All he had to do was sneak up on him and push him over the edge. But as Stryker watched, he saw the man pull on the rope, and a woman appeared on the other end.

He recognized her. She had been on Lopel too. Something was glowing in her hand. Stryker screamed and started running, vaguely aware of the cry of dragons heading his way. All he could think of was getting the pendant. After that, all would be well.

****

"Now?" Wren asked Udore.

Used to the mountains and knowing the shortcut to where they were going, the two guards had arrived just minutes before Stryker. After hearing the guard's report, Udore sent them back down the mountain to the village.

What was going to happen was not something that they could help with, but Ian, Rose, Joseph, and Fionn would need assistance if things didn't go as planned.

Udore knew that Sawdi was almost there and that Suzanne would be fighting as a dragon. Udore had hugged her and wished her well before she ran off further into the woods so that her transformation would not bring attention to the rest of the group.

Suzanne was sorry that there hadn't been time to say goodbye to everyone, but they all knew how she felt about them. But she had come to Thamon to help and protect her sister. Perhaps that was what her life had been about all along.

As she ran, Suzanne thought about her friends in the Earth and Erda Realms. She had been blessed to be able to live two full lives. When she had stepped through the portal that would bring her to

Meg on Thamon, she knew that she wouldn't be able to return. But given a choice again, she would do the same thing.

She had watched her sister transform into a woman who was willing to sacrifice everything for the people of Thamon. But that didn't mean that Meg had to die. Meg and Tarek could remain on Thamon after it was free from Aaron-Lem. If there was any chance that Meg would succeed in destroying the pendant and the ring that Sawdi wore, she would do everything that she knew how to do to make sure that happened.

From just a few miles away, she heard Bolong call to her. This was her destiny. To fight beside the man who had arrived in her life. Perhaps too late for both of them. But at least they would be fighting and, if necessary, dying together.

Behind her, she heard Wren ask again, "Now?" and Udore's answer, "Yes, Now."

She knew what that meant. Wren, Karn, Udore, and Silke had stepped out into the clearing to help Meg and Tarek. They were powerful. They were on the side of good. It had to work. It would work, or they would all die trying.

****

"Stop!" Udore yelled, raising his hand. A blast of energy hit Stryker as he ran. He staggered and fell. Lying on the ground, he lifted his head towards the sound. What he saw wasn't possible. Udore, not in his prison cell, standing with Karn. And that woman he had met at the rebels' headquarters on Lopel. And that Okan was sitting on Udore's shoulder.

How did these people get here? Hadn't the Warrior Monks and Sawdi destroyed them? Had he misjudged all of this? But even if he had, all he had to do was get the pendant out of that woman's hand and put the pieces together.

What had once seemed so easy now seemed almost impossible. Almost. But he could still do it. Stryker stumbled to his feet and started running again, barely registering the sound of dragons coming his way.

Udore shook his head and froze Stryker in his tracks. What happened next, only Meg could do. All of them watched as she stood on the edge of the cliff, staring at the thing glowing in her hand.

"You can do it, Meg," Udore whispered.

FIFTY FOUR

M eg didn't hear Udore. She didn't hear anything. All she felt was the power of the pendant. It was hers. She reached out her hand towards Stryker, frozen in the clearing, and pulled the pendant off his neck and ripped it out of his pocket.

She knew it wasn't her pulling the pieces together. It was something so much greater. She was one with the pendant. It had waited for eons for someone to put it together, and claim the power over Thamon, maybe even the Galaxy.

When Tarek reached out to her, she pushed him away. It didn't take any effort at all. She just thought No, and Tarek fell. Stryker was frozen, unable to move. The pieces of the pendant were moving towards her.

In the clearing, Meg could see the people called Udore, Wren, Karn, and Silke. She remembered them. But what did they matter? She could do whatever she wanted to do.

In her hand, the ruby glowed, pulling at the other parts of itself.

Above the woods, dragons were heading her way. She didn't care. They could be controlled too, including the man riding them.

And yet, the pieces remained suspended in the air as Meg, the woman from Erda, fought to remember.

****

Joseph and Fionn stood at the door of the Temple, watching the sky. The fire still raged on the mountain. Worry about the

Sanctuary and the people filled their hearts. Their friends had gone there. Did they survive?

There was nothing they could do about that, or what was coming. They could see the dragons in the distance, and they knew where they were heading. Sawdi was heading for their friends on the mountain.

Behind them, Ian knelt, his head bent to the floor. His daughter Rose had her hand on his back and her head on his shoulder. Her touch and her breath on his neck calmed him. He needed to remain calm. All his attention had to be on supporting the fight going on all over Thamon.

Although the future of Thamon rested in the hands of one young woman on the mountains not far away, it was what was happening in the rest of Thamon that would support her success, or not. Part of him wished that they could have told her what was going to happen. However, that would only have eased their minds and would not have helped her.

The fight she was fighting wasn't just for her, it was for everyone, but she had to find the answer for herself.

Ian breathed in and out. He thought of the people on the mountain supporting Meg. Of Baywolf, Ruth, Roar, and Dax at the Palace. Of his granddaughter, Iris. Of the women and children still in hiding on Edes.

He thought of the people in the Sanctuaries all over the world, especially the one that Sawdi believed he had destroyed on the mountain outside of Yeal Thalor.

Did his brother, Jori, and the people survive?

Ian thought of his son, Ibris, and the people on the Islands. Did they know that all these lives hung in the balance? Were they helping?

Ian thought of all the rebels: the Mages, shapeshifters, wizards, Ordinaries, even some members of the Kai Via and Preachers, who were waiting for the sign—waiting for Meg.

Ian knew that the fight was not with the men, Sawdi, Aaron, and Stryker. If they made the fight about people, they would not win.

That would be a fight that would never end. No, this was about defeating the real enemy. Ian was sure that was the mistake they had made in the past. If history was being repeated, then it was because they had missed the true meaning of what they were fighting.

Not people. But the desire to be powerful, to choose greed instead of equality. That desire took many forms, depending on who gave in to it. But it was evil. It destroyed and cared only for itself. However, fighting it with evil would only give it more power.

Would Meg see that? She had to this time. Ian joined the thousands of people praying all over Thamon to know that evil could not convince anyone, anywhere, to choose it. No names were mentioned. No one was blamed. Only love poured forth. It was hard work fighting the urge to hate or be afraid. But they did it.

Even those who did not know what was happening felt the wave of prayer passing through Thamon. They joined in.

Captain Lira, on the Eos in the harbor on Turva, knelt on the deck and prayed. Captain Kosti sailing towards the Islands turned towards Edes, not knowing why, but thinking he would be needed there, stopped and bowed his head. Not towards Aaron. But in support of whoever was fighting for the right for all people to think for themselves and be free.

Above them all, the suns crossed. Today, there was no blue flash. Meg had not yet chosen.

FIFTY FIVE

D ax and Ruth stared at Baywolf.

"You have a solution for the Warrior Monks?" Dax demanded. "How would you know what to do? Isn't Sawdi the only person who can control them? And he isn't here."

Baywolf chuckled. For the first time in his life, he was the one who knew more and was in charge. It was a lovely feeling, but not one that he was going to let linger. He had watched Aaron for too long and seen what the desire to be the all-knower did to him.

No, Baywolf wanted more. Perhaps he would never have it even if he did do the right thing. But at least he had a chance.

Baywolf answered Dax with a smile in his voice. "It's not Sawdi that controls them. It's the ring he wears."

"Well," Dax snorted. "Zonking good that does us. He's not here."

Baywolf didn't say anything. Just stood against the wall with his arms folded. Maybe they aren't smart enough to figure this out, he thought. Perhaps I'll have to do this on my own after all.

But Ruth started laughing, and Baywolf sighed in relief. He didn't want to do it by himself, and he liked this Ruth person. He couldn't remember his mother, but he thought she would be much like this woman. Maybe when this was all over, if they succeeded, she would help him find his family if they were still alive.

Ruth smiled at Baywolf, and he knew that she understood. A piece of his heart started to melt. Yes, he had made the right choice.

"What are you laughing about?" Dax demanded. He had been pumped up to get rid of Aaron, had decided to die doing it, and now this big hulk and this old woman were bonding? What was up with that? Where was the fight? He needed to fight.

Ruth reached over and touched Dax on the shoulder. She knew he didn't want anyone to hug him.

"If the ring is not here, Dax, then what is controlling the Warrior Monks?"

"Nothing?" Dax said.

"Fear," Ruth answered.

"So, are you saying we can walk out of here and do what we need to do with Aaron, and the Warrior Monks won't care?"

"Oh, they'll care. The Monks are programmed to do whatever they can do to make us afraid of them. But all their power will be in how we respond to them. If we fight back, they gain more power."

"Okay. Don't get it," Dax said, barely controlling his irritation. Why did people have to talk in riddles? Why not just go get Aaron and be done with it.

"We are going to be invisible to them," Baywolf said, and Ruth nodded.

"Exactly how are we going to do that?" Dax demanded.

"We are going to put on cloaks that make us invisible," Baywolf said.

"Where are we going to get those?" Dax snorted.

Ruth tapped his head and said, "It's what we'll be thinking."
****

On the Islands, the people had gathered in the Market and waited for the Preacher to arrive. Although he had asked them not to call him Preacher anymore, habits die hard, and that was his skill after all.

216

But now, at least they knew who he was. He was Ibris. And they had discovered he was a wizard. Many of them had been angry when they first learned of his deception.

But Oiseon and Samis had spent time among the people and explained to them why Ibris had done what he had. Some of the people understood. Some did not. But all of them were afraid. They knew that the only thing keeping the people of their Islands safe were the Mages and Ibris.

So despite some of their misgivings, when the call went out to gather at the Market, they stopped whatever they were doing and came running.

This time when Ibris spoke, there was no Kai-Via behind him. Once again, the crowd was divided. Most were glad they were gone, but there were a few who wished the Kai-Via were still there.

They missed the services. Even after being told that the water in the chalices and the pool had been drugged, they didn't care. They had felt better then. They didn't have to think so much.

But the majority of the people standing in front of Ibris knew that they had been liberated and were grateful, and it was to them that Ibris spoke.

It was a simple request. Ibris explained that at that very moment, across Thamon, a battle was being fought, and their help was needed.

Not to pray against someone, hate them, or fight anyone, but to see the bigger force that ruled Thamon.

They all experienced it every time they looked at a loved one and knew they were connected forever. They experienced it as they stood on the beach and watched the waves, or in the woods and witnessed the miracle of trees. They experienced it when a child took their hand in trust.

They all knew that feeling. What Ibris asked them to do was find that feeling and expand it. Let it dissolve anything that didn't feel the same way.

It was a simple request. Could they do it? Would they?

As the crowd bowed their heads, holding hands, a loud shout went up from the back.

Two men pushed their way through the crowd heading towards Oiseon, Samis, and Ibris. Their faces were red with anger.

"You are taking away our God. Aaron is God," they screamed. A few other men joined them, pushing aside anyone trying to stop them from reaching the front of the room, and a struggle broke out.

Ibris looked at Oiseon. The exact opposite of what he had asked from the crowd was happening.

Oiseon knew that Ibris was struggling with himself. There was truth in what the men were shouting. Ibris thought that maybe all of what they had done was in vain. Fear and greed would win again, and he felt that he was to blame.

Oiseon knew that if Ibris didn't snap out of it, and control his thinking, the moment would be lost, and it would be lifetimes before they had another chance.

Meg needed help now. A few seconds more and it would be too late.

FIFTY SIX

"Are you ready?" Baywolf asked Dax.

Dax thought it was a stupid question, but at a glance from Ruth, he tried to answer as politely and calmly as he could that he was trying to be.

Ruth and Baywolf exchanged looks. It would have to be enough. They had to go now. Both of them could feel the forces gathering all over the Island. They could use it to do what they needed to do. They had explained it to Dax, and he had laughed.

"You both sound like the Preacher. Are you sure you're not just spouting words that Aaron made up?"

Baywolf had put his massive hands on Dax's shoulder, leaned down, and said, "Fear, Dax. That's what you are feeling. You think that light, or love, or whatever you want to call good, is not stronger than fear.

"That's what it wants you to believe. But, you have overcome fear in your life many times, and this time you are doing it for all the right reasons."

Dax nodded, and asked, "But I plan to kill Aaron. How can that be right in your grand scheme of good?"

Ruth smiled at Dax. "Are you sure that's what you need to do? Yes, we do have to stop him. But how that happens, let's find out."

Dax shrugged. What else could he do? If he had to kill Aaron, he would, and no one could stop him.

Baywolf turned and walked through the wall, and after exchanging nervous glances about doing the same thing, Dax and Ruth followed him.

"I didn't feel anything," Dax said. "How can that be happening? Wouldn't I feel myself walking through the door?"

"But there isn't a door," Baywolf said. "It's an illusion. See?"

Dax turned and looked at the wall, seeing a wide-open space that had once been a wall of stone.

"It was never there?" Dax asked, thinking there was something important here for him to understand.

"It was never there," Baywolf confirmed.

****

Aaron watched the three people make their way through the Palace.

It was so shocking he didn't know what to do. First, what was Dax doing here? Who was that woman? And why was Baywolf with them?

To make it even more bizarre, every time they passed a place where he had hidden a tube, Baywolf smiled and waved.

Baywolf smiling? Aaron wasn't sure he had ever seen that before. It made his ugly face look almost appealing. And he was waving? How did he know about the tubes?

It was apparent that they were heading toward him as if they were all friends, and they were stopping by for tea. But it couldn't be that, could it? Aaron felt for the weapon hidden on his wrist.

He supposed that if it all came to that, he could use it on them. But after all the years training Baywolf, turning him to ash would be such a tragedy.

Dax and the woman, not so much. Then it occurred to him that perhaps Baywolf was bringing Dax to him so that he could kill him, and let Baywolf take his place.

With that thought, Aaron relaxed a little. That would explain what they were doing here. How they had gotten into the Palace was another question, though. How did they get past the Warrior Monks? Why weren't the Monks reacting to their presence?

So many questions needed to be answered, but Aaron was sure that Baywolf would fill him in.

Aaron turned to the Blessed One, waiting to be told what to do, and ordered him out of the room. He didn't want anyone to hear what was going to happen.

Besides, he was running low on Blessed Ones, and he couldn't get out of the Palace to find more. Because of the Warrior Monks keeping guard, he hadn't even been able to search for his women. Perhaps Baywolf could help with that.

There was a gentle knock on the throne room door. The Blessed One opened the door, as Aaron arranged himself on his throne. Yes, Dax and the woman were going to see him, but they wouldn't be living long anyway.

His three guests moved into the room as the Blessed One closed the door behind him, hiding a small gasp of surprise at what he saw.

Yes, he could see. Before leaving, Udore had restored as many Blessed One's sight that he could. He had been one of the lucky ones.

Ruth turned to him as the door shut and nodded. He knew the sign. It was time. He had to get to the rest of the Blessed Ones. They all had to do what Udore had told them to do. Pray.

Pray for the light to be stronger than the darkness. Send strength to the Chosen One, even now making a decision that would impact all of Thamon.

No longer pretending to be blind, he ran, not afraid, straight through the Warrior Monks who never saw him. Baywolf was right. Without the ring, and without his fear, they didn't know what to do.

In the room, Dax, Ruth, and Baywolf stood in front of Aaron. Only Baywolf was smiling. It was only then that Aaron realized that he might have been wrong. About all of it.

But before he could raise his arm, Ruth shifted into a raven and plucked the bracelet off his wrist and dropped it into Baywolf's hand.

Even then, Aaron could not believe that anyone would confront a god, and he was God. He refused to bow down to fear.

Dax turned to Baywolf and said, "Is it time?"

"Yes," Baywolf responded, "But not for what you think."

FIFTY SEVEN

Time had stopped. The pendant pieces hung in the air. Meg stood, her hand extended, the pendant piece in her hand burning, waiting.

Stryker, still on his knees, stared in horror at Meg. Stared at the two pieces of the pendant hanging in the air. Two pieces on the way to snapping together with the third piece in Meg's hand. When that happened, Meg would have the power that he had searched for and desired all his life.

Above Meg, five dragons were frozen in the air. Sawdi's ring was glowing, his face was distorted with the desire to stop Meg.

Meg didn't see any of that. She only felt the opposing desires fighting within her. The desire to be all-powerful and the desire to remember something. But what?

Unknown to Meg, across Thamon, people had gathered to support this moment. Most of them didn't know Meg or the battle that was now frozen in time.

Instead, they had heard the call to stand together in light. To proclaim the overreaching power of good to overcome anything unlike itself.

Not everyone heard that call in the same way. For some, it was a pause in their day to be grateful for the blessings in their life. For others, it was the moment they chose to love instead of hate.

But others knew what was going on in Turva. They felt the intense fear of what could happen and what it would mean to the people of Thamon, and they overcame that fear with love.

On the Islands, Ibris opened his arms to the men rushing the stage.

In the palace, Aaron was frozen in place.

Udore stood in the field, holding time still.

All of them, waiting.

Out of the stillness, a shriek rose from the woods, piercing the sky and Meg's heart, and releasing her from the frozen time.

Hand still reaching for the pendant, the pendant pieces still hanging in the air between her and Stryker, Meg turned her gaze to the sky.

Streaking across the blue sky, was her beloved sister, who always protected her, flying as Lady the dragon straight at the five dragons above her.

And on one of those dragons sat a man, who, like Stryker, had only one thing on his mind. Get the pendant.

****

Bolong heard Suzanne's call. She had come. Still frozen in time, Bolong could feel Sawdi and the ring pulling at the pendant. Bolong knew that if the ring and the pendant came together, all would be lost.

It was the moment that they had waited for. Using the energy Suzanne was sending, Bolong unfroze himself and the other four dragons. They had a plan in place, and it was time to do it.

Bolong rolled. Sawdi screamed and held on.

Below him, Bolong glanced down and saw the pendant fly into Meg's hand and snap itself together. It was as if what had slowed down time, now sped it up.

Meg stood with the pendant in her hand, feeling the power that it gave her. And she was glad. She loved it. She never thought she would feel this way. Nothing could ever harm her again. One thought, and she could control everyone and have anything she wanted.

She smiled. She knew exactly what she wanted.

Meg turned to her friends running to her and froze them in their tracks with just one thought. She didn't need them.

She watched as the dragon she knew to be Bolong turned over and over again, trying to throw that man Sawdi off of him.

Sawdi's ring was fighting, aiming red beams at the dragons that surrounded Bolong, ready to keep Sawdi from getting to her.

Meg smiled. That sister of hers, what a fighter.

As she watched, Sawdi's ring shot two dragons, and silently they started falling out of the sky.

That's enough, Meg thought. Give me the ring.

A split second later, the ring was in her hand. All she heard was Sawdi screaming, her sister crying, the world's heart breaking.

In that split second, when Meg grasped the ring, Udore thought, not again. Not again. He closed his eyes, waiting for what he knew was coming.

Meg, the wild-child from Erda, would unwittingly destroy every living thing on Thamon as she chose power over love.

Tarek stood beside his father, watching the love of his life close her hands over the ring and the pendant, and smile one last time before bursting into flames.

"Now," Karn yelled and ran towards Meg. Wren, Tarek, Silke, and Udore followed, forming a circle around her, standing so close their clothes and hair started to smoke. Still, they stood.

Tarek could see Meg standing in the flames with her eyes closed, hands clenched, the ring in one hand. The pendant in another.

"You can do it, Meg," Tarek whispered.

A split second later, the fire transformed into a beam of light. It shot out from Meg and branched out across the sky, through the trees, down in the canyon.

It found the falling dragons and held them.

It touched Sawdi, and he screamed and fell off Bolong, and the light let him go.

Stryker, seeing the light coming for him, covered his eyes, trying to escape, fearing what it would do. Instead, it passed gently through him, leaving him lying on his back, staring at the sky as if he had never seen it before.

On the Islands, the men rushing Ibris fell to their knees along with everyone else, as the light streaked through the sky just as Etar and Trin crossed paths. The resulting flash of light was seen all over Thamon.

Outside the Palace, the white mass of Warrior Monks melted, but not before releasing a deep sigh that sounded to those who heard it like a sigh of relief.

Inside the throne room, both wrist bands fell onto the gold floor, merging with the rainbows of light passing through the stained glass windows. Rainbows danced off the walls.

Aaron sat down. It was over. No one needed to tell him. His heart seized, and he fell off the throne.

Dax fell to his knees and wept.

Hidden away, in a cave, Jori watched as the book of prophecies burst into flames. It was over.

Fifty Eight

M eg collapsed into Tarek's arms. In her hands, the pieces of the pendant and the ring had turned to ashes. Her hair had turned white.

"She's not breathing," Tarek screamed.

It was Wren who pulled Meg from Tarek and said, "Go back to the Islands, Tarek," before flashing away with Meg.

Tarek screamed, "No!"

It was Karn and Udore holding on to him that kept Tarek from throwing himself over the cliff, trying to follow where Wren had gone.

It was only after he calmed down that Tarek realized that Silke was gone, too. "Now, what do I do?" Tarek moaned to Udore and Karn as they looked over the canyon.

All the dragons had disappeared from the sky, including Suzanne. There was nothing to see. Sawdi had fallen to the bottom of the gorge, and Stryker was lying lifeless on the grass.

"She saved Thamon, but did she have to die doing it?" Tarek cried.

Udore didn't have the heart to answer him. There was nothing he could say, anyway. He was just as much in the dark as his son was.

The prophecy had never gone past warnings. All they could do was follow what Wren had told them to do. Go back to the Islands.

But first, they needed to check on the Sanctuary and then the Temple.

Udore turned to his son and said, "If Meg were here, what would she have you do?"

Tarek didn't answer him. Instead, he thought back to the first time that he had seen Meg. He relived the moments they had spent together and how he had grown to love and admire her as she transformed herself.

As hard as it had been for her, Meg had as gracefully as possible let go of all that she had once valued about herself. And in the process become who she was.

In his heart, Tarek knew that she would tell him to do what he was meant to do. He had gone to the Islands to stop Aaron-Lem from taking away the freedom of the people.

Now that their liberty had been restored, the least he could do was help them rebuild their lives, rejoice in the ability to think for themselves, and choose the lives they wanted to live."

"She would want me to be helpful and feel joy."

Udore smiled and said, "Shall we go see our families?"

"Are you telling me that the people in the Sanctuary survived?"

"Of course they did," Karn answered. "Don't you think we had plans in place? The prophecies didn't tell us what would happen, but it did warn us.

"Besides, Bolong's dragons would never have set people on fire. My guess is that our friends and family are on the way to Yeal Thalor. Shall we go?"

It wasn't until they were on the Islands that Tarek stopped to think that Karn didn't seem that upset that Wren was gone too. It took many months before he knew why.

****

Before leaving the clearing, Tarek, Karn, and Udore buried the body of Stryker. All three prayed that Stryker had found peace at the last minute, so that his next life would be one filled with love rather than the need for power.

As Karn predicted, all the people from the Sanctuary were in Yeal Thalor, and the town was in a state of celebration. As the three men approached the village, a great roar went up from the people as they rushed to embrace them.

Tarek and Udore united with their families who had learned that they were still alive when Gelon and the Mages arrived months before. More news had come with Leon and the men from the ships. Everyone in the Sanctuary had prayed for their safety.

For days, the families and the rebels stayed and talked together. Stories of their years apart were shared. But as little time as possible was spent talking about the things that had separated them.

Finally, at the end of the week, Captain Lira said he was ready to leave. He had stayed off the seas long enough. The sea was where he belonged, and now that Thamon was free, he wanted to return to it.

On his first trip, he would go to the Islands and take everyone who wanted to go with him.

The next morning, everyone gathered in the harbor where the Eos was waiting for them. All of Lira's crew was ready to go, except one who decided to stay, having fallen for a local girl.

Although Joseph and Fionn were returning to the Islands, Leon and the rest of the men were staying with their families.

All of Tarek's family, including his father Udore, was staying on Turva. Udore said that he never wanted to leave his wife's side again. Tarek understood.

Now that Thamon was free, Udore said that they would come to visit when they could. They knew that Tarek needed to return to the Islands.

Most of the refugees from the Islands were returning on the Eos. However, Gelon and his family decided to stay, having fallen in love with Turva, too.

Jori, Ian, and Rose were torn between going to the Islands, or back to Edes. Tarek suggested they come with him. They could go to Edes after that if Dax and Iris weren't there.

Tarek thought that if Ruth, Roar, and Dax had survived their encounter with Aaron, they would return to the Islands and bring Iris with them. After a little persuasion, Jori, Ian, and Rose had agreed.

It was a time of both rejoicing and sorrow as they said goodbye and boarded the ship. Udore had hoped that the missing people would return before they left. But they didn't.

Sawdi's dragons and Suzanne were also still missing. Did the death of Sawdi kill them too?

In the quiet nights, as they made their way back to the Islands, Tarek prayed that he would find all of them where they were going. He knew that Suzanne loved the Islands, and would return there if she were alive. He wondered if Suzanne knew that her sister was gone.

Although Tarek was determined to fulfill Meg's desire for him to be happy, his heart was still broken. And to make matters worse, the string that tied him to Silke was no longer there.

The best way he could describe how he felt was untethered and empty. He thought he would never feel grounded again.

But perhaps if Suzanne was on the Islands, they could comfort each other.

It was that thought, and the stars at night that Meg had loved, that kept him going through the weeks as they made their way back to the Islands.

That and the small hope that Karn knew something Tarek didn't know, and that was why Karn only seemed lonely, not broken, like himself.

FIFTY NINE

T he three men sat on the bench on Hetale's beach. Not the three men who had wanted to rule the world. Three men who had done what they could to save it.

As they did every morning, Tarek, Ibris, and Karn sat together, watching as Trin and Erda moved across the sky. Watching the waves roll in and out as they had always done, as if nothing had changed. And yet everything had.

Months had gone by since Meg's light had flashed across Thamon. Months since Meg, Wren, Silke, Suzanne, and the dragons had disappeared.

Months where Tarek wept at night, knowing he shouldn't, that he knew better. But it was as if a piece of himself had broken off and fallen into the canyon that day.

Jori, Ian, and Rose had come to the Islands, but the ship they expected never arrived. Dax, Ruth, and Roar had not returned. They could only hope that they, and Iris, were safe.

Because although the dark force that had fallen over Thamon was lifted, no one on the Islands knew what had happened to Aaron in Edes. Was he still alive?

Falcon, who used to bring the news, was missing, too. Ibris wondered if he and the dragons were dead or transformed back to who they used to be. Either way, no one knew where all of them had gone.

Captain Lira had remained on the Islands for months, waiting for the Soleis. But now that the cold season was returning, Lira said that he and his men had to go. They would take Jori, Ian, and Rose to Edes. It was time. They couldn't wait any longer. They would leave the next day.

None of the men sitting on the bench watching the waves move in and out said anything to each other. All three of them were lost in their thoughts.

Tarek had tried countless times to ask Karn why he didn't seem broken, but Karn would only shake his head and walk away. Sometimes Karn would remind Tarek that Wren told them to meet her on the Islands. But that was all he would say.

Karn's belief that Wren would return gave Tarek the little hope that sustained him each day. That and the work that they had done together to help the people of the Islands.

The three men had supervised the building of a new Temple, but not for any specific religion. It was open to anyone to worship any god that they wished to. Ibris still preached, but he taught how to use the power of imagination towards positive outcomes and not to control others as Aaron-Lem had done.

The Temple was full every day. Everyone was welcome, even those who still worshiped Aaron.

It was a beautiful day, not quite cold, but a brisk wind warned of the coming cold season.

As the suns crossed and the blue light flashed, Karn stood. Tarek looked at him and was astonished to see tears running down his face. Never, after all that had happened, had Karn cried. Not once.

"What's wrong?" Tarek asked.

It was Ibris who pointed out what Karn had seen. Something in the distance. Tarek's heart started beating faster, but he didn't know why. Squinting against the suns, Ibris saw something that seemed impossible. Seven dragons.

As they got closer, Tarek saw why Karn was crying. Seated on one of the dragons with a long red stripe down its side, was Wren. He recognized it as the dragon called Bolong. Ruth was on another. Tarek knew it had to be Roar.

But it was the dragon with a red streak on its head that made him fall to his knees. Lady. And on her back was a woman waving to him. Meg had come home.

****

Of course, the Eos didn't leave the next day as planned. Instead, they stayed to celebrate the return of Meg, Roar, Ruth, Silke, Suzanne, and Wren.

But three days later, Rose, Jori, and Ian boarded the ship and headed to Edes.

Ibris and Tarek stood on the shore for a long time, watching them until they disappeared over the horizon. After hearing what was happening on Edes, they both knew that they might never see them again. But now that they knew that their families were safe, they could let them go.

Although everyone had been hungry to find out what had happened, Ibris had stepped in and insisted that the travelers rest first. Besides, Ibris knew that Karn and Wren, and Tarek and Meg were not interested in talking to anyone except each other.

All the dragons, touching down on the shore, had shifted back into the people they once were. However, they were no longer boys. They were now men.

Suzanne was their spokesperson. She did her best to answer questions, explaining that the men had been captives of Sawdi.

He had placed a spell on them to keep them dragons. The destruction of the ring had set them free. Falcon was also free, but he had stayed on Edes with Dax and Baywolf to help the people adjust to being free again.

That's all anyone knew until Wren called a meeting of the Mages and the rebels. They met at the building they had stayed at on Lopel.

It seemed a fitting place for them to catch up with each other and talk about what each group didn't know, like what happened on Edes or on the mountain.

While they waited for the meeting to begin, Karn and Bolong clapped each other on the back. Their plan had worked. And they both had lived. It was just one of the many celebrations that happened that day.

However, Tarek had hoped that they would also learn where all the missing people had gone after Wren took them away.

But Meg had told them it was up to Wren, whether she explained or not, and wasn't it enough that they had returned?

Tarek hugged her and answered through his tears, that it was.

SIXTY

Silke snuggled into Meg's neck. It was a special day. She wondered if there had ever been a day so glorious in all the years that she had lived. The cold season had come and gone. Once again, the people of the Islands met each day in the Market.

She and Meg went every morning. But now Meg didn't have to hide who she was or steal food to stay alive. She couldn't have hidden if she wanted to. Everyone knew her. But not as the woman who had saved them and fulfilled a prophecy, but as Tarek's future wife. And that was the way she wanted it.

It was Wren who had done that for her. First, she saved her and then hid what had happened, so that Meg could live an ordinary life, at least for a while, on the Islands. It was what Meg wanted, and Meg was grateful to Wren.

Only a few people knew what happened that day on the mountain. Everyone else had forgotten. Wren had seen to that, too.

Meg was no longer a shapeshifter, and she couldn't have been happier. She loved watching Suzanne and Bolong play above the Islands as dragons but felt nothing but happiness for them.

Today was a special day for everyone. Today they were waiting for the Eos and the Soleis to return to the Islands. The two ships were bringing their friends and family to a celebration.

The Soleis was bringing Dax along with Rose, Ian, Jori, and Iris. Baywolf and Falcon said they could hold Edes together if Dax wanted to leave to see his cousin and friends married.

After the light flashed, and the wrist bands fell to the floor, both Dax and Aaron had collapsed. Baywolf had taken them to the Blessed Ones, where they were cared for despite what both of them had done.

Dax had recovered and, for the first time in his life, found a measure of peace. By the time Jori, Ian, and Rose arrived on Edes, Dax was busy helping Baywolf and Falcon return Thamon to how it was before Aaron, Stryker, and Sawdi decided to run it.

Although sometimes Dax still felt restless, he didn't turn that into violence. Instead, he and his father worked with other members of the Kai-Via, who were recovering from Stryker's training. Knowing that his father, Jori, was proud of him, went a long way towards Dax's recovery.

Aaron never fully recovered. All his riches and power were gone. Both Stryker and Sawdi had died, and now that they didn't influence him anymore, he became a shell of the man he used to be.

In a fitting turn of events, the women he had abused, and the children he planned to turn into his private army, cared for him. They built a small cottage for him in the middle of the garden, and Aaron seemed quite content to sit and watch it grow.

Ian had restored sight to the rest of the Blessed Ones. Most of them wanted to keep the scar on the shoulders where Sawdi had stabbed them to test them.

They didn't want to forget. They vowed never to let something like that happen again on Thamon. And even though there were still those that worshiped Aaron, not wanting to give up their beliefs, they were free to do so. But not control others in the process.

The Eos was bringing Leon, some of his men, and Udore and his wife, for the ceremony.

The two ships arrived early in the morning, both ships helped along by the wizards on board. By the time the Eos and Soleis started lowering rowboats filled with the visitors, a crowd had gathered. Silke sat on Tarek's shoulder as they watched their families come ashore.

As soon as everyone greeted one another, and rivers of happy tears were shed, the entire crowd moved to the Temple where the Mages had been busy setting it up for the ceremony.

Today would be a day like no other. Not only would Tarek and Meg be married, but Wren and Karn were renewing their vows, and Suzanne and Bolong would also wed.

Ruth and Roar were in charge of everything, which was what everyone wanted. Every Islander was invited. The Mages were in charge of making sure there was enough food, Samis and his friends were in charge of making sure everyone found a place to stand or sit.

This was not just a wedding. It was a celebration of the power of love, diversity, and community.

At midday, Ibris stood in front of the crowd. Behind him stood seven men, all of them smiling. They weren't the Kai-Via or the Preacher. They were friends of the wedding party.

Wren and Karn, Tarek and Meg, Suzanne and Bolong, stood in front of Ibris and the seven men from their families, and said their vows. Above them, the blue light flashed, and the people of the Islands cheered.

****

Later, after the crowds had gone, the three couples and Silke sat together on Ibris' favorite bench. The night was clear, and the stars filled the sky.

No one spoke. Their hearts were full of the love that had been shared that day.

It was Meg who asked the question. "Will we be staying?"

Wren looked up at the sky before asking, "How many places do you think those brothers did those experiments?"

No one answered because no one knew the answer.

What the seven of them did know was that someday they might have to find out.

In the meantime, the Islands were their home. And today was the beginning of the rest of their lives together.

WHAT'S NEXT

T hroughout the *Chronicles of Thamon* series, there were references to the lives that Meg and Suzanne had before coming to Thamon.

If reading this series has aroused your curiosity, you might try out my fantasy series called *The Return To Erda,* where Suzanne first learned about the bored brothers. Erda is also where her friend Hannah, aka Princess Kara Beth, defeated them.

If you would like to start at the beginning, try *Stories From Doveland,* a Magical Realism series set in contemporary earth time, where you will meet characters that you will encounter in my other series.

Suzanne references this time in the Earth Realm as the time when she was an ambassador between the Earth and Erda dimensions.

If you join my mailing list at becalewis.com/thamon, you can get the free short story that answers so many questions about how the Karass, Erda, and Thamon series are related. Yes, Suzanne is in all of them. How is that possible?

And, as you noticed, this book leaves open a few questions.

Where did Wren take Meg and Silke? What happened there? And will the seven explore other dimensions and planets?

If you sign up for my mailing list and/or follow me on your favorite author platform, you will be the first to know the answers to those questions.

AUTHOR NOTES

I was editing this book as the coronavirus first hit the world.
Within days, my life, like yours, was entirely different from just
a few months before when I started writing *Discovered*.

Then I was writing in various coffee houses as I attempted to get
away from my home, which called me to do the laundry or read
another book instead of writing one.

I would go very early as it opened. Often, I was the only one there
for the first few hours, which was fine with me.

However, even though I got lost in the world of writing, I would
often overhear conversations, and sometimes that conversation
would spark an idea that ended up in the book—like the name
Meg—yes, named after a lovely barista at my favorite Starbucks
store.

Every book tells me more about myself.

I discovered, as I wrote my first fiction novel, *Karass*, that my
point of view that shows up in my non-fiction, spiritual self-help
books (*The Shift Series*), could not be shut off as I thought it could.

The characters reflected what I believe about the forces of
good and evil. Or more accurately, how Good is the only power.
Everything else that is not in harmony with the idea of consistent,
universal, and infinite good dissolves.

But we each have to choose to make that stand within ourselves,
and in the end, it is never a fight with someone else.

That's why, as much as I think I want to have one, there is never a traditional battle scene. I try to write them. In this book, I planned to write one towards the end. But no.

As the words flowed out onto my keyboard, I found I was ending the book—once again—with the "good" guys choosing another way to dissolve the evil that had taken over their world.

Every day, we all have to make this kind of choice. Is it possible to stop greed and power for power's sake without fighting it? There has to be a way to do it. Otherwise, this battle will continue forever.

In my books, I get to work it out. Some people will say, well, it's fantasy after all. Is it?

I don't think so. It's up to us to be the light that dissolves all darkness. Easy to write about in a book, harder to put into practice. Even so, it can and must be done. See, there's my point of view right there.

And now, at home, in the middle of a pandemic, I see it is even more important to remember this Truth.

Standing with you, my dear reader, as we choose light.

Yours, Beca

ACKNOWLEDGEMENTS

I could never write a book without the help of my friends and my book community. Thank you, Jet Tucker, Jamie Lewis, Diana Cormier, and Barbara Budan, for taking the time to do the final reader proof. You can't imagine how much I appreciate it.

A huge thank you to Laura Moliter for her fantastic book editing.

Thank you to every other member of my Book Community who help me make so many decisions that help the book be the best book possible.

Thank you to all the people who tell me that they love to read these stories. Those random comments from friends and strangers are more valuable than gold.

And as always, thank you to my beloved husband, Del, for being my daily sounding board, for putting up with all my questions, my constant need to want to make things better, and for being the love of my life, in more than just this one lifetime.

Also By Beca

The Rivers of Time Series: Women's Lit, Friendship, Small Town, Mystery, Magical Realism, Small Town Fiction
The Returning, The Awakening, The Rising

***Follow Me Here:* Women's Lit, Friendship, Small Town, Mystery, Magical Realism, Small Town Fiction**

The Ruby Sisters Series: Women's Lit, Friendship, Mystery, Small Town Fiction
A Last Gift, After All This Time, And Then She Remembered, As If It Was Real, Almost Innocent

Stories From Doveland: Women's Lit, Friendship, Small Town, Mystery, Magical Realism, Small Town Fiction
Karass, Pragma, Jatismar, Exousia, Stemma, Paragnosis, In-Between, Missing, Out Of Nowhere

The Return To Erda Series: Fantasy
Shatterskin, Deadsweep, Abbadon, The Experiment

The Chronicles of Thamon: Fantasy
Banished, Betrayed, Discovered, Wren's Story

243

The Shift Series: Spiritual Self-Help
Living in Grace: The Shift to Spiritual Perception
The Daily Shift: Daily Lessons From Love To Money
The 4 Essential Questions: Choosing Spiritually Healthy Habits
The 28 Day Shift To Wealth: A Daily Prosperity Plan
The Intent Course: Say Yes To What Moves You
Imagination Mastery: A Workbook For Shifting Your Reality
Right Thinking: A Thoughtful System for Healing
Perception Mastery: Seven Steps To Lasting Change
Blooming Your Life: How To Experience Consistent Happiness

Perception Parables: Very short stories
Love's Silent Sweet Secret: A Fable About Love
Golden Chains And Silver Cords: A Fable About Letting Go

Advice / Journals
A Woman's ABC's of Life: Lessons in Love, Life, and Career from
Those Who Learned The Hard Way
The Daily Nudge(s): So When Did You First Notice

About Beca

Beca writes books she hopes will change people's perceptions of themselves and the world, and open possibilities to things and ideas that are waiting to be seen and experienced.

At sixteen, Beca founded her own dance studio. Later, she received a Master's Degree in Dance in Choreography from UCLA and founded the Harbinger Dance Theatre, a multimedia dance company, while continuing to run her dance school.

After graduating—to better support her three children—Beca switched to the sales field, where she worked as an employee and independent contractor in many industries, excelling in each while perfecting and teaching her Shift System and writing books.

She joined the financial industry in 1983 and became an Associate Vice President of Investments at a major stock brokerage firm. She was a licensed Certified Financial Planner for over twenty years.

This diversity, along with a variety of life challenges, helped fuel the desire to share what she's learned by writing and speaking, hoping it will make a difference in other people's lives.

Beca grew up in State College, PA, with the dream of becoming a dancer and then a writer. She carried that dream forward as she fulfilled a childhood wish by moving to Southern California in 1968. Beca told her family she would never move back to the cold.

After living there for thirty one years, she met her husband, Delbert Lee Piper, Sr., at a retreat in Virginia, and everything changed. They decided to find a place they could call their own, which sent them off traveling around the United States. They lived and worked in a few different places before returning to live in the cold once again near Del's family in a small town in Northeast Ohio, not too far from State College.

When not working and teaching together, they love to visit and play with their combined family of eight children and five grandchildren, walk, read, study, do yoga or taiji, feed birds, and work in their garden.